THE MARINE'S E-MAIL ORDER BRIDE

CORA SETON

The Marine's E-Mail Order Bride
Copyright © 2014 Cora Seton
Print Edition

ISBN: 9 78-1-927036-68-6
Published by One Acre Press

AUTHOR'S NOTE

The Marine's E-Mail Order Bride is the third in the five volume series, **The Heroes of Chance Creek**. To find out more about Mason, Regan, Austin, Zane, Colt and other Chance Creek inhabitants, look for the rest of the books in the series, including:

Find out where it all began with **The Cowboys of Chance Creek** Series:

Visit www.coraseton.com for more titles and release dates.

Sign up for my newsletter here:
www.coraseton.com/sign-up-for-my-newsletter

CHAPTER ONE

O F ALL THE things she'd done as assistant to mountaineer Kenna North, this was certainly the strangest, Storm Willow thought as she climbed the outside stairs to the second floor of the Big Sky Motel. Located in tiny Chance Creek, Montana, it was a nondescript building whose windows overlooked a parking lot in what passed for a downtown area. Flying in from California, she'd watched the large, sparsely populated ranches spread out below her as the plane descended to the airport. To the southwest had been a tall range of mountains. The town itself was barely visible until they were almost over it. It looked snug and self-reliant tucked among the open spaces surrounding it, so different from her bustling seaside hometown, Santa Cruz.

Too bad she wasn't the one getting married in the fancy white gown encased in the garment bag she was hauling up the motel's outdoor stairs. Her last boy-friend, Todd Winters, had crushed any aspirations she had in that department when she'd brought up the topic in the spring. She could still hear his response.

"Marriage? For God's sake, Storm, we're twenty-three. No one our age gets married. We're supposed to have fun and be spontaneous, but you wouldn't know anything about that, would you? Your life is scheduled six months out. You can't even spend the night with me without checking your date book!"

They hadn't lasted long after that, and no one else seemed eager to step into Todd's shoes. Now it was September, and she hadn't had more than a date or two in the meantime. What hurt the most was that Todd was right; there was no time for spontaneity in her life. Her father had died when she was fifteen, and with three much younger sisters to help care and provide for, she'd jumped right from junior high to parenthood. Now she worked full time, ran Zoe, Daisy and Violet to their activities and watched them every Saturday so her mother could take extra shifts. She was responsible. That didn't mean she was boring. She too longed for adventure—someday, but when it came she wanted someone to share it with. Was that really so bad?

She moved the heavy garment bag to a new position and kept climbing. Todd's words had hurt, but they'd also confirmed something she'd long suspected. Men these days didn't know how to grow up. They bumbled around and acted like children long past their teens and into their twenties. Take Todd, for example, who worked as few nights as possible at a dance club so that he could spend his days surfing. That was great as far as it went—her own father had a terrific career in surfing that allowed him to buy the beach cottage she still lived in with her mother and sisters—but at some point you had to have a plan. Todd wasn't Mitch Willow. He wasn't going to get a surfing sponsorship. He was going to wake up one morning at forty-four and realize he'd missed his chance to own a home or start a family.

She wanted a home and family, but she wasn't interested in dating any more boys. In fact, she'd written men off altogether for the time being. She'd decided the only way out of her current situation was to concentrate on her career and figure out how to turn this position with Kenna into something more—something that would actually pay all her bills and allow her to pursue some of her own dreams. Maybe then she'd be able to meet a man who was her equal, a man capable of acting like an adult.

Storm negotiated the last few metal stairs, surveyed the numbers on the motel room doors and turned left. As sick as she was of men right now, she was even more tired of being in debt. It wasn't the gas bill, or medical insurance or keeping food on the table that was the problem.

It was the house. The beautiful cottage Mitch had bought when he made his first big splash as a professional surfer. Right on West Cliff Drive, with the best ocean views around, it was a spectacular home, and every time Storm entered it she was reminded of her father's love for them all.

Unfortunately, when Mitch died in a surfing accident in Bali eight years ago, he hadn't only left Storm's mother, Cheyenne, four girls to raise, he'd also left her an enormous mortgage. Within months, Storm had quit school to work full-time, but with the cost of daycare for a three-year-old and one-year-old twins, plus an outsized house payment, her earnings paired with Cheyenne's couldn't keep up. Cheyenne took a second job while Storm struggled to get her GED. When she looked back, she realized together they'd pulled off a miracle holding onto the house and keeping themselves above water—barely—this long. Each year they'd slid a little bit, however, and now their debts had become too big to ignore. Something had to change.

But not today.

She paused in front of number twenty-seven. Kenna should already be in the next room over, but Storm wanted one last minute to herself before she informed her of her arrival.

She couldn't believe Kenna was getting married—to a cowboy, no less. Every time she thought about it she had to laugh. Kenna was tough as nails, a no-nonsense climber who had no time for sentiment or romance. A cowboy was entirely wasted on her.

Of course, it would be a fake wedding. Kenna would never agree to be shackled for long. Storm had been with her the day her father's will had been read, and Kenna had found that she wouldn't receive her substantial inheritance until she was married. Storm had thought her boss might explode when she got the news, but instead Kenna had gone quiet, and had stayed subdued until she left a few days later for Nepal for her latest climbing expedition. Storm should have known she was formulating a plan.

She draped the garment bag over her left arm and fumbled with the key she'd received downstairs at the check-in counter. Kenna's wedding dress had arrived in the mail two weeks ago with orders for Storm to get it here. As Kenna's assistant, it was her job to do all kinds of things. She kept Kenna's home running during her months-long excursions, helped write her grant requests and climbing articles, kept her books, coordinated her travel arrangements and anything and everything else Kenna wanted done. Kenna knew Storm would never say no to a job—Storm needed the money far too badly to jeopardize her position—so she didn't hold back on her requests. In turn, Storm knew just how badly Kenna wanted that inheritance. The fact Kenna had used the Internet to find herself a fake husband shouldn't have surprised her one bit. For the next six weeks it would be Storm's job to pull together the wedding here in Chance Creek and stand in as Kenna's best friend and Maid of Honor. Another laugh. Kenna made sure she was always aware of the discrepancy between their positions. There was nothing resembling friendship between them.

The key turned in the lock and Storm let herself in, hung up the dress in the closet, and flopped down on the bed, exhausted. Ever since Kenna had informed her of her upcoming wedding, she'd been on her feet, rushing to prepare for her trip to Montana. She'd done everything she could to make her prolonged absence easier on her mother. She wasn't sure how Cheyenne would manage to work full time, do her errands and get the girls where they needed to go while she was gone.

As much as she hated to admit it, Storm was looking forward to the break. She loved her family, but Todd was right about one thing—her time never felt like her own. She'd be plenty busy helping Kenna arrange her fake marriage, but when she wasn't working, she could relax and think about the future—especially about how to find a better-paying job.

Or how to convince Cheyenne to sell the house, so all her decisions didn't have to be based on money.

A knock on the door startled her, and she put a hand to her chest, willing her heartbeat to slow. Kenna must have noticed her arrival and wondered what was taking her so long.

Six weeks, she reminded herself as she walked to the door. She could endure anything for six weeks, even catering to Kenna's every whim as she prepared for her fake Thanksgiving wedding to a cowboy who apparently needed a temporary wife as badly as Kenna needed a temporary husband. She wondered what the man would be like. Probably ugly, she decided, if he couldn't find a willing woman. Buck-toothed, maybe. Illiterate, perhaps. Fond of words like *howdy* and *school-marm*. As lazy and boyish as Todd.

The knock sounded again.

"I'm coming." She'd better take that annoyance out of her voice or Kenna would have something to say about it.

Her phone shrilled out the sharp, insistent ring she'd programmed to announce that her boss was calling. Storm grabbed it out of her pocket automatically even though she was sure she was about to come face to face with the woman. Kenna demanded absolute attention from her employees. If she called, you answered, even if she was simultaneously knocking on your door.

"Hello?" She rested her hand on the knob.

"Storm? You'll have to take my place."

Storm frowned at the urgency in her boss's voice. "Take your place? Where?"

"In Chance Creek. You're there, aren't you?" Kenna's frustration was evident.

"Of course I'm here. I'm about to let you into my room." Storm was sure her own frustration was all too clear.

"That would be a trick, seeing as I'm still in Nepal."

"What?" Storm took a step back from her door. "What are you doing there?" She strode back to the bed where she had Kenna's itinerary in her bag.

"I got delayed. I'm not going to make it back—there's a new expedition setting out and I've been invited to join it. It's too good to pass up."

"What about your wedding?" Was Kenna joking? Storm had just thrown her life into an uproar to get here.

"That's what I mean—you'll have to take my place."

Storm pulled the phone away from her face and

stared at it. Lifting it back to her ear, she said, "What are you talking about?"

"You'll have to be Kenna North for the next six weeks. All you have to do is hang out with the cowboy, marry him at Thanksgiving, stay a couple more days and then leave. I'm supposed to be going to the Andes then, anyway. No one will know the difference."

"Your husband will!"

"Don't play dumb. You know as well as I do there's nothing real about this marriage. Zane doesn't care who the bride is. He's seen one photo of me—tell him it was an old one. Say you've grown out your hair."

"That's insane!" Kenna was five inches taller than Storm and could probably bench-press her, too. Every inch of Kenna was muscle. Her features were much stronger than Storm's. Apart from the fact they were both blonde, they didn't share more than a passing resemblance.

"It'll be fine."

She had to be kidding. "What about my ID? The minute he sees my driver's license, he'll know I'm lying."

"I've already taken care of that. Your new identity is on its way. You'll get an envelope by the end of the day. Zane's got the marriage license and we've both already signed the pre-nup, so you don't even need to worry about that."

"You're buying fake ID's now?"

The knock sounded at the door again.

"Someone's here," Storm told Kenna. "Is that the

courier?"

"That's your husband. Go answer it."

"No! Kenna, no—I won't do it. No way. This is crazy."

"Ah, but it's lucrative, too."

Storm stood still. "How lucrative?" She hated herself for even asking.

"Thirty thousand dollars lucrative. All you have to do is pretend to be me for six weeks, marry him and leave. I'll take care of the rest. You'll get a check the minute I receive my inheritance. This is important," she added when Storm didn't answer. "This climb—it's the chance of a lifetime for me."

Storm sat down on the bed. Thirty thousand dollars? Enough to pay off all their debts with a little left over?

She couldn't say yes, though. She couldn't perpetrate a fraud.

"Zane Hall wants a fake wife as much as I want a fake husband," Kenna said. "He has to fool his family into thinking he's getting married to inherit the ranch he lives on. He's in exactly the same position I am—and he's under a deadline. Come on, Storm. You can do this."

The knock came again.

"I'll probably end up in jail," Storm said finally.

"You won't end up in jail. Let me make this simple for you. Marry the cowboy or lose your job. I'll get in touch when I can." Kenna cut the call.

Storm lowered the phone slowly and faced the

door, her thoughts too tangled to make sense. A fake marriage? Six weeks? Thirty thousand dollars? As she debated her options, a single image came into her mind—her mother and sisters standing in the doorway of the seaside home they loved so much, waving goodbye as she left in a cab for the airport. She knew what Cheyenne would want her to do. Marry the man and get the cash.

Storm wasn't wired that way, though. She was law-abiding. She did things honorably. That's why she hadn't skipped out on her mother even when friend after friend told her she was crazy to stay at home and help raise her sisters instead of leaving and starting her own life when she turned eighteen.

She'd always taken the high road and she wasn't about to change that now. Storm squared her shoulders. Kenna would have to come home after all. She'd tell the cowboy her boss had been delayed and call Kenna back and demand she get on the first flight out of Nepal.

She pulled open the door, and the words she had prepared to say died on her lips. Outside stood the most handsome man she'd ever seen. He was six foot two, she estimated, with shoulders wide enough to support a world of cares. His features were strong, his hazel eyes frank but intelligent. He wore jeans that were worn to a comfortable fit, and a forest green, button-down shirt layered over a white T-shirt. As she stared at him, transfixed by his easy smile, the strong line of his jaw, and the flash of interest in his eyes when he saw her, he touched the brim of his cowboy hat. "Hi, I'm Zane Hall," he said in a voice that held just a hint of a western twang.

"Hi," she heard herself answer. "I'm Kenna North."

ZANE HALL BREATHED a sigh of relief when the motel room door finally opened, relief that turned to shock as it revealed a young woman with blue eyes and a sheet of blonde hair flowing to her waist. She was petite, delicate, with a mouth made for kissing and a curvy figure that had all his senses perking up despite his resolutions not to fall for his temporary bride. Sheer surprise had him grinning as he touched the brim of his hat.

Kenna North was a knockout. He hadn't been prepared for that.

She was far prettier than Julie Simpson, the woman who'd driven him to choose this fake marriage rather than searching for the real thing. When he'd learned last spring that he and his brothers had a chance to inherit Crescent Hall, the family ranch they'd had to leave years ago, he'd felt like he'd been given another lease on life. He'd already planned to leave the Marines in the fall. Going home to Montana and working the spread with his brothers had been a secret dream of his the entire twelve years they'd been gone.

Then he learned the catch. Among other requirements, he and his brothers all had to marry within the year. They'd decided the prize was worth it. His oldest brother, Mason, and Zane's twin, Austin, had both used the Internet to find wives and were now happily married. He'd thought he'd be able to do it, too.

He'd been wrong.

He'd used the Internet in a slightly different way than his brothers had. The original ad Mason had placed for all of them hadn't produced any candidates who interested him, so he'd looked up a woman he'd known in the early days of his military career. A fellow Marine, she'd only been stationed with him for a short time and while they'd flirted shamelessly during that period, he'd been too conscious of the dangers of fraternization among the ranks to act on his attraction. He figured it was a connection worth pursuing now, however, given the short time-frame he had to work with.

Julie Simpson answered his first message eagerly and soon they'd gotten in the habit of texting daily and calling when they could. She'd been stationed at Camp Lejeune while he was finishing his time in the military at Camp Pendleton, but that didn't curtail their communications. Their conversations ran from politics to military tactics, with a heavy dose of silliness and sexual innuendo. Julie was shameless; she had no filters and would have him hooting with laughter and half-hard, all at the same time. He couldn't quite pin down what she felt for him, though. There was too much joking mixed up in her lustful texts to be sure.

After five or six weeks of bantering and feeling her out to make sure there wasn't a boyfriend lurking in the wings, Zane finally asked if she'd like to try to spend the weekend together if they could arrange time off simultaneously.

Julie hadn't answered for three days.

By the time he received her next text, he'd beaten himself up ten ways from Sunday for being an ass and a fool. He wasn't sure if he'd jumped the gun or if Julie thought they were still simply pals from boot camp. Her answer explained everything.

"You do know I'm gay, right?"

He hadn't had a clue. It was his turn not to answer out of embarrassment that he'd read the situation so wrong, but she'd called and kept calling until he finally picked up.

"Seriously, Hall? You thought I was hitting on you?"

"I hoped you were." He'd tried for a light tone but wasn't sure it had worked. Their correspondence had tapered off, and he'd been back to the starting point. With only six months left to beat Heloise's deadline, he'd decided a fake wife was the way to go. He couldn't risk any more surprises.

His new wife-wanted ad made it clear the marriage would be a business transaction plain and simple. Unfortunately, the answers he'd received were enough to turn his hair white—until he got a matter-of-fact note from Kenna North, mountain climber, whose father obviously felt the need to meddle in her life the way his Great Aunt Heloise felt the need to meddle in his.

In order to secure a substantial inheritance, I need a fake husband for a period of six months, most of which time I'll be out of the country on climbing expeditions. My demands are few. I need proof of the marriage, a water-tight pre-nup, and your agreement to divorce without contest when the six months are up. If you can keep your demands similarly reasonable, we may be able to make a deal.

He had kept his demands as reasonable as possible. Six weeks on his family's ranch to establish that she was indeed his willing fiancée, before a Thanksgiving wedding attended by all his kin. After that she was free to leave for her next climbing trip. An appearance or two when she was back in the country until the six months were up, by which time his aunt would have signed over the deed on the ranch to him and his brothers.

It was all very simple. Cut and dried. Just the way he wanted his love life from now on until he had more time to dedicate to the process. The next time he proposed to a woman, he'd have lived with her for at least a year, he promised himself—long enough to know all her secrets. No one would catch him off guard again.

The woman framed in the motel room doorway had him reevaluating all his plans. This wasn't how he had pictured Kenna at all. From the little her photo had shown he'd imagined her as tall, muscular and matter-of-fact. What happened to her spiky haircut? Not that he missed it. Not one bit.

"Hi, I'm Zane Hall," he said finally.

"I'm Kenna North." She peered up at him, seeming as surprised at his appearance as he was at hers. He'd thought the photograph he sent her was a fairly good one, but maybe he'd been wrong.

"Can I come in?"

She hesitated, her gaze flicking over him. Zane stilled. Was she judging him? What would she do if he wasn't up to snuff? His family was expecting to meet her tomorrow and he didn't have a backup plan if she cancelled the deal. They didn't know she had flown in today to spend the night in town. Kenna had demanded a grace period to make sure he wasn't an axe murderer, as she put it, or otherwise unsuitable to masquerade as her husband temporarily. It had seemed like a reasonable request at the time.

Now all he wanted to know was how soon he could get her into his bed.

Zane caught himself. Wait... no. That wasn't what this deal was about. He was done rushing into relationships. In fact, Kenna herself had been all too clear that touching each other was off-limits, save for the few kisses they'd need to share in public to fool his family.

He was suddenly looking forward to those kisses.

"How about we go for a walk instead? I've been sitting all morning," she said. "Let me get my purse."

"Okay." He put his hat back on and waited, giving himself a mental talking-to. Ten seconds in Kenna's company and he was ready to renege on all the promises he'd made himself? Kenna was a very temporary bride and she was entirely unsuitable for him to pursue. She had made it clear her life was mountain climbing. She traveled the world and came home just long enough to set up her next expedition. He was very clear that he wanted a wife who'd make a future with him here on the ranch. No more detours down romantic paths that couldn't work out. From now on he was waiting until he found a woman who wanted to marry and settle down right here as much as he did. "How were your flights?" he asked when Kenna returned. He looked her over again as she shut and locked the motel room door. Everything about her was overtly feminine. How had a tiny thing like her climbed all those mountains?

"Just fine." She seemed as nervous as he was as she led the way toward the stairs.

"Where would you like to walk?" he asked.

"Can you recommend a place?"

"I can show you downtown."

"Sure."

They were silent as they took the stairs down to the street, and Zane searched for something to say, distracted by her figure as she negotiated the steps in front of him. There was something soft and sweet about her that made him feel protective of her—which was silly. This woman had explored some of the most dangerous places on earth. "I'm glad you're here." He was surprised to find he really meant it. He *was* glad she was here. In fact, he was looking forward to getting to know her a whole lot better. He frowned. Damn it, there he went again.

"I'm glad I'm here too." She shot him a look over her shoulder. "I mean, it's strange but it's... better than I expected."

Was that a blush tracing over her cheeks? Zane's body responded with a throb of interest. "Strange because..."

She shrugged. "Meeting like this. Lying to people about the fact we don't even know each other."

Uh-oh. Was she having second thoughts? "I've done stranger things in the Marines. I'm sure you must have found yourself in some tight spots in the mountains."

She was silent a moment. "Oh... of course. The mountains. It's just." She waved a hand. "Marriage. That's a pretty big deal, isn't it?"

When he didn't answer, she glanced up again. They reached the bottom of the stairs and Zane led the way toward the street. "It is to me," he finally said.

"Really? Why did you agree to this, then?"

He frowned as they walked side by side. "Same reason you did. I want my inheritance."

"Oh. Right. Of course." She shrugged. "Sorry. Jet lag."

"Neither of us likes to lie, right? We've just been forced into it by our circumstances."

"You're right; I hate lying. Especially about marriage."

Taken aback by her vehemence, Zane digested this in silence, turning left at the corner in order to avoid the busier roads. He didn't want to risk one of his brothers driving by and spotting him with Kenna. They needed this chance to sync up their stories before he took her home.

Since he'd only been back in town for a week, himself, normally he'd have taken the opportunity to analyze the changes in Chance Creek during his long absence. Today his attention was squarely on Kenna, though. In her e-mails she had struck him as the most practical of women. He hadn't expected her to have qualms. Or to care about marriage.

"I always hoped I'd get married... for real," she confessed, keeping her eyes on the sidewalk. "I never dreamed I'd be faking it."

Her vulnerability pierced his heart. He'd never dreamed he'd be faking it, either. He had always seen himself as a family man, like his father. Recent events had made him wonder if he'd ever get to play that role.

"You'll marry again," he said and frowned at the stab of disquiet his words had caused him. At the moment, he didn't want to think of Kenna with anyone. Except him. He shook his head at his inability to shift his thoughts about her to a platonic place. Hadn't he learned anything from his experience with Julie? He didn't know this woman. He couldn't make any judgments about her.

"I never thought I'd marry more than once," she said quietly.

She could have sucker-punched him and it wouldn't have shocked him more. Kenna wasn't at all the hard-nosed, unfeeling woman he'd chalked her up to be. She was a true romantic.

She was looking for love.

Well, hell, so was he. He wanted to be married. He wanted to start a family, just like his brothers were doing. It was Julie's fault he'd put all of that off.

Had he given up too soon? The situation with Julie was one to laugh at, really—not one to make him turn his back on his dreams.

He looked Kenna over again.

Maybe he had given up too soon.

"What do we do next?" she asked.

He had to take a second to get his bearings. Do next? He could think of a lot of things he'd like to do next, but he couldn't suggest any of them to this delicate nymph. "I guess we get to know each other better."

CHAPTER TWO

S TORM WANTED TO get to know Zane better—a lot better. But how did you do that in the space of a single afternoon?

Walking sedately through the outskirts of the little town wasn't telling her much of anything. She knew he'd had a career in the military over a decade long, so she supposed he couldn't be a quitter. He held himself ramrod straight, which told her he was confident, but there was a hint of a sense of humor in the way he smiled at her that assured her he knew how to have fun. Still, that wasn't enough. She wanted to know everything about Zane Hall. She could barely keep herself from staring at him, and the butterflies in her stomach whirled every time he returned her gaze.

He pointed out landmarks to her as they went. The barber shop where he'd had his hair cut as a boy. A corner store where he'd bought comic books.

The first time their hands brushed as they walked, she felt a little thrill. The second time she wondered if that touch was deliberate. She slid a glance under her lashes at the man beside her only to find him looking back at her. A knowing smile curved his mouth and her breath caught in her throat. Was he flirting with her?

Their fingertips touched again and just for a second—a space of time so short she thought she must have imagined it—his fingers tangled with hers and gave her a little tug. She bit her lip as a jolt of desire ripped through her.

He was flirting with her.

Searching for something to say to cover her confusion, she nearly laughed with relief when they turned another corner and met up with a teenage boy walking two golden retriever puppies on a leash. Storm ducked down quickly and let the puppies sniff her hand. They practically fell over each other to butt her palm with their noses. She ruffled their fur, hoping that would give her the time she needed to figure out this latest turn of events. When she'd agreed to take Kenna's place she'd figured it would be a chore to pose as her boss. Zane had changed her mind in a heartbeat. Six weeks pretending to be his fiancée? Staying close to him? Holding hands? Maybe... kissing him?

Hell, yeah. She could do that.

Would he want to take things even further, she wondered, burying her face in the first puppy's fur. Just for the sake of authenticity of course—so they'd really *know* each other. She stifled a giggle. God, she was bad. There was no way she was going to sleep with Kenna's fake husband. It was absolutely out of the question.

Zane was chatting with the dogs' owner, thank goodness, so he hadn't noticed how hard she was blushing again. She couldn't help imagining what Zane's body would be like. How he would touch her, what it would be like to make love…

She stifled a groan. She couldn't even think like this. Zane was off limits. He was just a job.

"You don't mind us petting them, do you?" Zane was asking the boy.

"No, that's okay." Zane crouched down beside her. "Just watch out—Lance is a…" The teenager laughed when one of the puppies jumped right up on Zane. "He's a climber."

"He sure is." Zane tousled the dog's fur and scratched behind his ears until the puppy was in a paroxysm of happiness. Lance licked Zane's face while the other puppy tried to find a way to join his friend. Dancing back he leaped up and bowled Zane over. Zane sat down hard on the sidewalk and laughed. "They're a handful."

"Sorry. Ben, get down. Ben!"

You can always tell what a man's like by the way he treats his pets. Storm blinked when her father's voice rang through her mind. When had Mitch said that? One day when she was eight or nine and they'd been walking along West Cliff Drive, coming home from surfing. They'd seen a man be cruel to a dog and Mitch had intervened, first filming the incident on his waterproof camera, then threating to send the movie to Animal Welfare. That was her father all over, champion of the weak.

"No problem, don't worry about it," Zane said.

"They're good dogs, yes they are." As he rubbed and petted both of them, crooning a kind of baby talk they seemed to love, Storm's heart melted. If you could tell a lot about a man by the way he treated pets, then Zane was a caring, happy, friendly man.

The kind of man she'd always wanted to meet.

Stop it, she told herself sternly. She didn't need a friendly man. She needed one who stepped up and took responsibility when the chips were down.

Twelve years in the Marines, a little voice said. Didn't that suggest Zane could be responsible when the situation called for it?

She wasn't sure what happened next. One minute both puppies were climbing all over Zane. The next minute Lance spotted a Corgi being walked across the street, tugged free of his collar and made a break for it.

Instantly, Zane leaped to his feet, spilling Ben to the sidewalk. Before Storm could call out, Zane had given chase. He caught up to Lance just as a truck screeched to a halt to avoid hitting the puppy. The driver slammed a hand on his horn. Zane stood his ground, scooped Lance up and gave him a once over before turning to come back.

"That's the second time he's gotten free," the teenager said, hurrying to meet him. "Lance, what are you thinking?"

Zane helped the boy get the dog's collar back on. "See, here's where it's defective. You'd better get him new one before you take him out again."

"I will." The teen pet Lance a couple

as if to prove to himself his dog was really all right. "Thanks. I'm going to take them home."

"Sounds like a good plan." Zane turned back to Storm as the boy walked back the way he had come. "Sorry about that. Should we get some lunch?"

Sorry about that? The man was apologizing for what he'd done? She could only nod. She'd gotten her answer. Zane was responsible. He wasn't afraid to put himself in danger if it meant protecting someone—or something—else. He wasn't at all like Todd.

"You could have gotten hurt."

"Nah. There's not much traffic in Chance Creek."

All it takes is one car, she wanted to say, but didn't. He didn't want her to make a big deal out of it. Brave, responsible, caring and humble.

A dangerous combination.

"Look, we shouldn't eat at a restaurant since you're not supposed to be here yet. How about I walk you back to your motel and go grab some takeout. There's a new place that's half Mexican, half Afghan food. Fila's. It's pretty good." He took her hand as if it was the most normal thing in the world and led the way. Storm allowed herself to appreciate the feel of a warm, strong male hand wrapped around hers. His palm was calloused from work and the size of his hand made her feel delicate. She fought an urge to lean against him and increase the intimacy of the gesture. She didn't know how a man she'd just met could affect her so deeply, and she tried to match a word to her emotions. She'd been attracted to men before, of course, but she had never felt such raw hunger for one. She wanted more of him—much more.

Lust, she thought. *This is lust*. Pure, unbridled, unstoppable lust. The combination of Zane's strength and kindness had touched off a firestorm of desire in her she didn't know how to quench. From the glances he shot at her from time to time, she'd say she wasn't the only one affected by the touch of their hands.

They didn't speak much as they made their way back to the motel and up the stairs to the second floor.

"Kenna, can I ask you a question?" Zane stopped outside the door to her room.

"Of course." No matter where her gaze rested, the Marine was fascinating, from his direct gaze, to the curve of his smile to the hollow at the base of his throat.

"When you realized what you had to do to get your inheritance, what did you feel?"

Storm searched for an answer. Kenna had been furious, of course, but she couldn't say that to Zane, not when the way he was looking at her told her he too was struggling against a current of desire.

"You know what I felt?" he went on when she didn't reply, and his deep, warm voice touched off a new wave of want within her. "Relief. I wanted to marry anyway, but I was beginning to think I was the only one in the world who felt that way. The guys in my unit acted like marriage was a death sentence. Even the women I met seemed to think that." He shrugged. "You'd think no one believed in marriage anymore. I do, though. I've always known exactly what I want. To get my family's ranch back, to fall in love with a beautiful woman, and to start a family with her. When I heard Heloise's conditions for inheriting the ranch, I thought, 'Well, now I've got an excuse for going out and getting a wife.'" He laughed, but it was a bitter sound. "I've never told anyone that." He looked away and the brim of his hat hid his face from view for a moment. When he turned back toward her his gaze was direct and searching. "What about you? Have you ever wanted something like that?"

Storm barely trusted herself to answer. Kenna would say no—she'd never wanted a husband or a family.

But Storm wasn't Kenna.

"Yes. I've always wanted to marry, too. My parents were so happy together and it's been so hard on my mom since…" She caught herself just in time, realizing she was getting her story crossed with Kenna's. "I've always wanted to marry. I want…" What did she want? "I want a partner in life. Someone I can depend on. Someone I can celebrate with when things go well. I want us each to have our separate passions, but I want us to have plenty that we do together, too. Does that make sense?"

"That makes perfect sense. Kenna, I—"

"Call me Storm," she said on impulse. "All my friends do." Each time he said Kenna's name it felt like a slap to the face. She didn't want to remember Zane was her boss's pretend fiancé, not hers. She didn't want to think about Kenna at all.

"Storm," he said slowly. "I like that. It suits you better than Kenna. Storm, I feel like you and I—" He broke off, turned away, and surveyed the parking lot beneath them. "Never mind. Come on. Let's get you inside and I'll be back in a minute with some food."

Disappointment stabbed through her. What had he been about to say?

She forced the feeling down, and told herself to stop being such a fool. There could be nothing between her and Zane, even if he was saying all the things she'd always longed to hear from a man. She had to keep things on an even keel. She was here because it was her job to be here—because Kenna would pay her to do the job well.

If Zane ever found that out, she could kiss him good-bye.

Of course, she'd have to kiss him good-bye anyway when her six weeks were up. Her heart ached at the thought of it, and she scolded herself for being foolish. She barely knew the man. She couldn't be falling for him.

But she knew she was.

WHAT THE HELL was wrong with him, Zane asked himself as he strode toward Fila's. He couldn't believe what he'd almost said to Storm back there. *I think you and I could make a real go of it.*

Really? He thought the woman he'd known for all of an hour was his soul-mate? In what universe was love at first sight even possible?

Not this one.

He had to stop hoping for that kind of connection and get to the matter at hand. In less than twenty-four hours he'd present Storm as his fiancée to his family, and they would live together with his brothers and their wives for the next six weeks. It was time for him and Storm to swap all the necessary details so they could act their parts. The rest of the afternoon was for home-work, not flirting.

Although flirting sounded like a hell of a lot more fun. Storm liked him; he could tell. When he'd taken her hand she hadn't even tried to tug it away. If she had, he would have let her, of course, and he would have kept their relationship as innocent as it had started. She'd let him hold her hand, though, and had seemed disappointed when he finally let it go.

What would it be like to kiss Storm? To do more than that?

Zane nearly sighed in frustration. It was too risky. He had to remember what was at stake here—the ranch he and his brothers all loved. If he scared Storm off now, he was in trouble.

Still, they needed to pretend they were in love. A little flirting couldn't hurt.

He quickened his pace.

When he arrived back at Storm's room a half-hour later, she gestured for him to set down the meal on the Formica table near the window. As he took his seat and unpacked the meal, Storm exclaimed over the entrees he'd chosen.

"This all looks delicious!"

"I told you. Do you like curry?"

"Love it."

"Beef or chicken?"

"Chicken."

He handed her a container and a piece of naan bread to dip into the sauce. "I guessed right."

"What about you? Beef or chicken?"

"I'm a cattle rancher. Beef, of course."

"Huh. Which do you like better? Hamburgers or steak?"

"You got me there. Burgers. Don't tell anyone, though."

"I prefer steak," she said.

"Ketchup or mustard?" he asked, playing along with the game.

"Ketchup."

"I like mustard. And relish."

"Bacon or sausage?" Storm asked, opening the container he'd passed her.

"Bacon."

"Me, too."

He leaned over and kissed her, then pulled back, as surprised as she was. "Sorry. Just seemed like the right thing to do somehow." He chuckled at her expression. She looked half-shocked, half-pleased. He had been about to say it wouldn't happen again, but he thought better of it. It just might.

"Beer or wine?" he asked to smooth things over.

"Wine," she said slowly, "although a cold beer on a hot day when you're exhausted from a long bike ride is pretty sweet."

"I prefer beer no matter what the occasion." They were back on solid ground and he took a few bites of his curry before he asked another question. "Zombies or vampires?"

"Neither." She made a face. "Surfing or skate-boarding?"

"I've never tried either one. Have you?"

"I'm terrific at surfing. Not so great on a skate-board."

He filed that information away. "How about ice cream? Chocolate or vanilla?"

"Chocolate, of course."

"Me, too," he said, glad they were back to common ground. Her silence caught his attention after a moment and when he glanced her way he found her watching him. Was she… waiting for another kiss? He didn't stop to think about it. He leaned over and snatched one before the moment was lost. "Mm, you taste like curry."

"You, too."

"Your turn."

"My turn?"

"To ask a question."

She took a bite, as if she wasn't fazed by this game at all, but her cheeks were pink and he could tell she was trying to think of a good one. "House or condo?"

He snorted. "House, of course. Wait until you see

mine. You'll love it." She would. Everyone loved the Hall. "Shower or bath?"

She choked on the bite she'd just taken and he pounded her back while she struggled to sip water from her cup. "That's pretty personal, don't you think?"

"We're going to be married in six short weeks," he reminded her. "I need to know these things."

Her color deepened. "Shower for getting clean, bath for relaxing."

"Same." He waited for her to turn his way again. This time as he bent to kiss her, he took his time, tilting her chin up with his fingers so she met him halfway. He lingered over the kiss, his lips sliding over hers, then deepened the connection, tracing his tongue over hers, tasting her. When he pulled back she bit her lip and played with her fork, not meeting his gaze.

"In the bath or in the shower?" he asked.

"What do you mean?"

From the way the flush spread over her cheeks he was pretty sure she knew exactly what he meant. "Where do you prefer to make love?"

Her eyes widened, then she quickly looked away. For a moment he thought he'd gone too far and he wanted to kick himself for spoiling the game before they'd hardly begun to play, but when he opened his mouth to apologize, she whispered, "Shower."

Heat rushed through him at the thought of taking her that way. He'd be able to see all of her—to feel all of her as he lifted her against the bathroom wall and thrust inside her, the steam from the hot water swirling around them.

He forced himself back to the present. He couldn't leave her hanging while he fantasized, not after she'd been brave enough to answer him. "Me, too." He set his fork down and cupped her chin with both hands as he bent for another kiss. Somehow he found himself on his feet, Storm rising with him and he pulled her into an embrace, no longer holding back at all. Storm felt good in his arms. So good.

"Tongue or no tongue?" he asked, brushing kisses down her neck.

"Tongue."

He rose up to capture her mouth again, cupping the back of her neck with one palm, sliding the other hand down her back. She kissed him back hungrily, twining her fingers behind his neck.

"Behind the ear or along the collarbone?" he asked.

"Collarbone."

He obliged, loving the taste of her. On fire with the knowledge that this game was approaching a line of no return. "Buttoned or unbuttoned?" he said, tugging at her shirt.

She hesitated and he waited for her answer, holding his breath.

"Unbuttoned." Heat surged through him as he bent to the task and quickly had her shirt undone. Beneath it her breasts were displayed in lacy cups that made desire pulse through him again. He swept a kiss from one soft mound to the other, lingering in the hollow between them. He was about to ask another question when

Storm spoke up.

"Bra or no bra?" she asked, burying her face against his shoulder.

"No bra." He pulled her shirt from the waistband of her skirt and slid his hands up to the clasp of the lacy garment.

"Me, too," she said and sighed when he undid the catch. He skimmed his hands under her bra and palmed her breasts.

"Hands or mouth?" he asked as he gloried in the sweet weight of her breasts.

"Mouth." She moaned as he made short work of her shirt, pulling it off her shoulders. He tangled his fingers in her bra and tossed it aside, then bent to take one nipple in his mouth. She clung to him, arching her back to give him greater access, working at the buttons on his shirt in turn. He pulled back, shouldered his way out of the button down and tugged his T-shirt off in one swift motion. "Looking or touching?"

"Touching." She smoothed her palms over his chest, then took his hands in hers and lifted them to her breasts again. He obeyed her silent request, tracing circles around them until he couldn't hold back.

"Standing or lying down?" He nudged her toward the bed.

"Lying down." She sat down on the mattress, pulling him down with her. He lifted her onto the center of the bed and climbed on top of her, kissing her again until they were both breathless. He allowed himself the chance to explore her fully, tracing kisses around the rosy peaks of her nipples, squeezing and feasting on them in turn as she moaned and gasped beneath him. When her fingers found the button of his jeans he stilled and pulled back.

Storm was every bit as beautiful as he'd thought she'd be with her blonde hair tossed in a halo around her face. "All or nothing?" she asked him in a voice so low he thought he'd dreamed the question.

Need pulsed through him again, hot and urgent. "All," he said and bent to kiss her, helping her help him tug off his jeans. He groaned when her hands plunged down under the waistband of his boxers, and made quick work of losing them too. He knelt above her, letting her take a good long look. "Skirt on or off?"

She bit her lip. "Sometimes on, but today off."

"Good answer," he growled and found the fastening behind her back. His fingers were clumsy, but soon he was sliding the soft skirt off of her, the sight of the one scrap of lace and silk still left between them only increasing his desire to know everything about her. As he tossed her skirt away he bent to trail a string of kisses from her breasts down to her belly. He knelt between her legs and eased her panties off. "Foreplay or main event?" He dipped down to kiss her in an intimate place and she sighed.

"Both?"

"Of course." He plunged his hands under her hips and lifted her to meet his mouth, eager to explore every inch of her hidden charms. Storm gasped beneath him, her fingers clutching the bedclothes. He asked no more questions, preferring to trust his instincts now. They didn't let him down and soon Storm was tugging at his shoulders, urging him back up to cover her.

"Slow or fast?" he asked when he'd found a condom in his jeans and quickly sheathed himself.

"Slow, then fast," she said, wrapping her arms around his neck as he took his place between her legs again.

Zane did as she asked, pushing inside her slowly, enjoying every sweet inch of wet pressure that surrounded him. He pulled back and pushed in again, watching her close her eyes, her face a study in ecstasy.

How had this miracle occurred, he wondered as he continued. What coincidence had brought Storm to Chance Creek, into his life, into his arms, exactly when he needed her most? The best of it was he was slated to marry her in six short weeks. Just when he thought he'd turned his back on the possibility of love, it had been handed to him as neat as a package.

Wonder overtook him as he increased his pace and her breasts rose and fell with his movements. He captured her wrists and plunged into her again, lowering himself to press against her fully. Every inch of her excited him where they touched, and though they were far from completion, he found himself dreaming of other positions to try on other occasions. He knew they would be together again—many, many times.

Storm's ragged breathing made him increase his pace again and soon he was plunging into her with an abandon that brought him close to the end. Her moans and cries told him she was close, too. Redoubling his speed, he thrust into her again and again until he swept them both over the edge. They cried out together and Zane held her tight until they were both spent. Collapsing on top of her, he pulled her over onto their sides, still joined.

"Once or twice?" he asked.

She laughed. "Twice."

This time when he kissed her, Zane took his time, letting his gentleness and insistence say what he wanted to say. He wanted to be with her. He wanted to get close to her. As he cleaned up, found a new condom and pressed inside of her again he hoped she understood.

This wasn't going to be a sham wedding.

He would do everything in his power to see if it could be real.

STORM LAY BACK and let Zane make love to her thoroughly, competently and so completely that she no longer knew where she ended and he began. When she came for a second time, calling out his name, she realized that she was in over her head. She was long past keeping control of the situation. Zane was calling the shots now.

At least she wouldn't have to pretend to his family that she knew him. She felt like she knew everything about him after their shared intimacies. She knew how his muscles were etched like stone when he flexed them. She knew how soft and tender he could be when coaxing her to open to him. She knew that he was generous, making sure of her pleasure before giving rein to his own.

She'd only met this man a few hours ago, and she was halfway to loving him. She'd never felt anything like this.

Never *done* anything like this. It was crazy to lie here with a man she barely knew and contemplate the marriage ahead of them. Was she acting so wantonly because she was far from home and none of this felt real?

Or had she really met the man for her in Chance Creek, Montana?

"What's going on in that pretty head?" Zane asked, brushing a kiss over her brow.

"I didn't expect... this."

"Neither did I."

"What do we do now?"

"I can think of a lot of things." He smoothed a hand down her hip. "But I'll have to get home before anyone starts asking questions I don't want to answer. I wish I could stay with you tonight."

"I wish you could too." But already reality was crashing in. She should be grateful he was going home. It would give her time to formulate a new plan. She couldn't go on lying to him—not when they'd connected like this.

She feared telling him the truth, though. How would he react?

Then there were her mother and sisters, who were counting on her to earn her bonus and get them up to date on their bills. If she told Zane the truth, she'd never get the money.

"What's wrong?"

She opened her eyes to find Zane staring at her in concern. "Nothing. It's just... I don't want to lose you," she said in a rush.

"You won't lose me."

She sat up, reaching for her bra. "This is only temporary. We both need to remember that."

"Maybe I don't want to remember that." He sat up too.

"Zane—"

"Shh." He held a finger to her lips, then kissed her quickly. "We'll figure it all out. There's no reason we can't."

She opened her mouth to speak again, then sighed when he tugged her bra away and bent to lavish attention on her breasts again. "Leave it all to me," he said a few minutes later. "I won't let you down, Kenna."

Storm blinked, her boss's name on Zane's lips like a dash of cold water to her face. What was she doing? She had to remember who was really marrying Zane.

But as he pulled her close to make love to her a third time, Storm let all her concerns slide away. She'd worry about Kenna tomorrow.

Today she was all Zane's.

When they'd exhausted themselves in bed, Zane

snuggled her under the covers and questioned her until they both felt they could do a creditable job posing as an engaged couple. The fact they now knew each other's bodies so intimately would go a far way to lending credence to the act. He knew just how to make her moan, and she knew where to kiss him to drive him wild.

They finished the rest of their food in bed and by the time they were done, Storm was beginning to feel adept at weaving the events of Kenna's life together with her own sensibilities and opinions. The fact that she handled almost every aspect of Kenna's calendar and day-to-day existence made the exercise much easier than it would otherwise be. In return, she'd learned more about the cattle ranch Zane and his three brothers had been given the chance to jointly inherit, and that it meant the world to Zane to succeed because he'd never wanted to leave it in the first place. She knew that his great aunt Heloise was a termagant of a woman whom they all feared to cross. She knew that his older brother Mason and his twin, Austin, already lived at the ranch—named Crescent Hall, after the house the family inhabited—with their wives, Regan and Ella.

She'd done her best to keep the conversation most-ly about him, deflecting his questions when they got too difficult to answer. She knew a lot about Kenna's climbing expeditions, having helped to plan them and edit the papers she wrote about them. She'd seen thousands of photographs of every trip Kenna had been on, but she'd never done more than some moderate hiking herself, and she didn't want to trip herself up.

From time to time, Zane touched her hand again, and another wave of raw desire crashed through her body. She'd never felt such an insatiable craving for a man. She knew she should worry about the future, but she found it hard to think of anything but the present.

He left when the sun was low in the sky, saying he had to be home for dinner or his brothers would want to know what had kept him away. She walked him to the door wrapped in her robe.

"I'll be honest—I never thought things would go like this." He let his gaze slide over her again, his appreciation all too clear. Storm knew exactly what he meant. She hadn't expected this either. "I'll pick you up at ten tomorrow morning," Zane went on. "My family thinks you're coming in on a plane. I've had a hell of a time dissuading them from coming along to greet you at the airport, but I told them you wanted a few minutes alone with me before they swamped you."

"Okay. I'll be ready." She wished he could spend the night. Already she was second-guessing herself. It wasn't that she regretted what they'd done. She didn't. She just knew it couldn't last, so maybe it would have been better never to have been with him at all.

He leaned against the doorframe a moment, searching her gaze before he reached out and tucked a strand of hair behind her ear. "Don't overthink this. I told you, it will all be okay. I'll see you tomorrow first thing." He leaned down to press a kiss to her mouth. When he pulled back, he chuckled. "Damn, Storm, you're a hell of a woman. I'd be honored to have you as my wife."

She swallowed hard as the quick grin she'd already grown to like so much returned to his face. She'd be honored to have him as a husband. A strong, handsome man who'd had the guts and determination to serve his country for over a decade? A man who'd go to such lengths to ensure the ranch he loved stayed in his family? A man who saved helpless puppies from certain death?

He was the polar opposite of child-like Todd.

"Thank you," she managed to say, wishing she could come up with something wittier. In a few short hours Zane had made her a believer again in men and marriage.

He saluted her. "Until tomorrow. Sweet dreams tonight."

"You, too. Good-bye."

She waited until he'd disappeared from view down the stairs, whistling, before she went inside, closed the door again and sank to the floor, dropping her head in her hands.

She wanted Zane more than she'd ever wanted a man in her life.

Too bad he could never be hers.

CHAPTER THREE

"I T'S STRANGE BEING home, isn't it?" Zane's twin, Austin, said to him later that night. They were sitting on the back porch of Crescent Hall, both wearing jackets against the chill in the September air. "Feeling any qualms about leaving the service?"

"Some." That was to be expected, though. The Marines had been his life for twelve years. He was proud as heck of the time he'd served, and he wouldn't give up a minute of it, but going home to Montana to ranch the property his forebears had carved out over a hundred years ago had always been his number one dream. His childhood seemed impossibly idyllic now. He and his brothers had lived and breathed cattle ranching under the supervision of their father, Aaron Hall, every day of their lives until Zane was seventeen. He'd thought he'd go on living right there forever—until his father's sudden death.

"The strangest part about coming home again for me was that Dad wasn't here to meet me." Austin took a swig from his bottle of beer and stared into the darkness beyond the porch lights.

Zane was too used to his twin reading his thoughts to be surprised at Austin's words. When the aneurysm struck down their father, their whole world had turned upside down. Completely unexpected, his passing left a hole in their family none of them knew how to fill. Seven days after his death, with the anguish of Aaron's funeral still fresh in their hearts, a knock came on the front door that overturned things again.

Zane had been halfway down the stairs when his mother answered it. The man standing on the front porch was almost as familiar as his father. Uncle Zeke had worked the ranch alongside Aaron, and was a daily presence in Zane's life, living as he did in a clapboard house on a separate parcel that bounded the property. Zeke had never been talkative and he certainly wasn't a cheerful man, but Zane hadn't minded that. With the self-absorption of a teenager, he'd never given Zeke much thought at all.

He realized right away that day something had changed. His mother must have too, because she stepped back without offering Zeke a greeting, the door still open wide.

"You know why I'm here," Zeke had said.

Something held Zane on the stairs when he wanted to go stand beside his mother. He didn't know what was happening. He just knew it wasn't good.

"Zeke—"

His uncle ignored Zane's mother's plea.

"I'll give you a week. That's it. I've waited long enough."

A week? Zane remembered his confusion at the time. A week for what? To mourn their father? To get back to work?

But already the truth was creeping over him.

A week to leave.

"Zeke, no!" His mother's voice was thick with tears. Zane had gripped the bannister so hard he thought he'd snap it, but he'd been raised to show the man respect. He didn't know what to do. Didn't know how to stop the nightmare unfolding in front of him.

"One week." Zeke put a foot on the threshold and Zane's mother shrunk back. "I've never said one word about the injustice of it. Now it's my turn to live in the Hall."

Only when his uncle turned to go had Zane spotted his cousin Darren standing behind him. He'd never forget the look on Darren's face.

Pure triumph.

Even now the memory had him balling his hands into fists.

"It feels good to be back, though," Austin said, interrupting his thoughts. "It keeps surprising me how it's different, but at the same time it's like nothing's changed now that we've gotten the place fixed up again."

Zane knew what his brother meant. Zeke and Darren had strutted around the place like a pair of peacocks during the family's last week there, acting as if they couldn't wait to run the place once Zane, his brothers and his mother packed their things and travelled to Florida to stay with Zane's aunt.

As soon as they were gone, however, Zeke and Darren showed their true colors. They let the place go. Darren moved out when the two of them quarreled a few years later. Zeke couldn't keep up with the work, and by the time he passed away the ranch had fallen into ruin.

"You and Mason did an excellent job," Zane answered his brother.

"All those years seemed like a long time when I was away, but now it feels like I never left. Not that I'm wishing away my time in the Army."

"Of course not." Although Zane knew Austin's last tour had been hard.

Once they moved in with their aunt, it had soon become obvious she didn't have room in her small house for four teenage boys. He'd never forget the day his older brother, Mason, called them together and told them his plan. Enlist in the service and make his own way in the world. It had made sense to Zane—to all of them. He and Austin had enlisted too, and Colt had followed as soon as he was old enough.

"I'll never forget the day Mason called and told us Crescent Hall was ours again," Austin said, breaking into his thoughts.

"Me, neither."

Six months ago, when Mason had summoned them all to a four-way video call to tell them Zeke had passed away and the ranch was theirs again, Zane had been so shocked he hadn't known what to say. It turned out

Zeke had never changed his will to leave the place to Darren. His old will stipulated the ranch reverted to their Great Aunt Heloise on Zeke's death, and she'd decided to pass it to Zane and his brothers.

He wondered what Darren thought about that. He'd never shown much interest in the ranching operation but he was married now, with a passel of kids of his own, and he must have wanted the house, at least.

Of course, there were certain conditions Zane and his brothers had to meet to get the spread. He shook his head. Any sane men would have run when they heard them, but the prize was Crescent Hall, one of the oldest ranches in Chance Creek, Montana. You didn't run from that.

Fix up the ranch and Hall—the three story, gray gothic mansion that gave the spread its name. Stock the ranch with enough cattle to make it a going concern. Get married and produce at least one heir among the four of them—all within the space of one year. Those last two conditions had caused quite a stir among his brothers.

"Can't believe I'm married, either," Austin said, right on cue.

Zane had to laugh. "Can't believe I'm about to be."

"I'm glad you've found the one," Austin said.

"Yeah." Zane took a drink from his beer, wishing it was that easy. As far as he and Kenna had taken things today—*Storm*, he corrected himself—he couldn't fool himself into thinking they'd live happily ever after just like that. His thoughts might have gone straight toward the long term, but that didn't mean hers had. For all he knew she saw him as a holiday fling. She'd talked a good game, but maybe that was all it was—talk. He took another drink. He had no doubt Storm would haunt his dreams tonight.

Three times they'd been together—each time better than the last. Already he wanted her again. This couldn't be some short-term thing.

He should have said something to Storm about it, but what? *Hey, I've known you for an afternoon and now I'd like to marry you?* He was sure that would have gone over well. Besides, they were getting married soon. He couldn't be the only one wondering if the terms of that wedding would change between now and then.

He'd better take this one day at a time, like he'd done with everything else since he'd learned they could inherit Crescent Hall. Heloise and her demands. He shook his head. She sure had him and his brothers jumping. They'd pitched in the money it had taken to get the ranch up and running again. Mason and Austin, who'd left their branches of the service sooner than he had, managed to fix up the barns, stables, outbuildings and the Hall itself. They'd stocked the ranch with cattle, horses and equipment to run it right. They'd both found wives, per Heloise's instructions, and Mason would be a father in March. They'd learned that Colt had a son, as well, from a teenage fling. Colt didn't know about his son yet—he was out of communication due to his current mission with the Air Force.

All that was left was for Zane and Colt to marry before Heloise's deadline. Colt had stated right from the start he didn't intend to leave the Air Force to ranch, but he'd promised to do his part anyway and get hitched.

Despite all his worries, contentedness filled Zane when he thought it all over. Family. He knew now it was all about family. The men he'd worked with were a kind of family too, but his career had kept him rootless, and he ached to build something permanent. He ached for the land he'd grown up on, the business he'd learned from the time he could walk. He longed to bring up his own family there and teach his own sons the way his father had taught him. He wanted to be surrounded by those who loved the ranch as much as he did—whose goals matched his.

He wanted a wife, too. A wife just like Storm. As soon as he'd gotten near her today, it had been all he could do not to wrap his fists in that hair of hers and tug her in close. He'd wanted to breathe in her California sun-kissed scent. He'd wanted to bury himself in that lithe, sweet body and forget all about the past.

He'd done it too. He couldn't believe it, but he had.

Three times.

Was Storm thinking of him now? Was she wondering all the same things about him he was wondering about her? It was more than just her body that enticed him. It was her desire for a home and family, and to create a life together with a husband. He'd begun to doubt women like her even existed. It was exhilarating to find out he was wrong.

Is that how she thought of him? He remembered how she'd clung to him when he'd pulled back from his last kiss. He shifted uncomfortably as his brother spoke again. "What's Kenna like?"

"She prefers to go by Storm," Zane began. "And she's... beautiful."

Austin grinned at him. "You got it bad, buddy."

Zane nodded slowly. His brother was right.

"How do you like Montana? Is it as awful as it sounds?" Cheyenne asked when Storm called her that night.

"It's pretty, actually."

"Ugh. I don't believe it. I bet it's freezing."

"Brisk, maybe, but hardly freezing."

"You wait, by Thanksgiving you'll be an ice cube."

"Let's hope for the best."

"How is Kenna? Nervous?"

Storm braced herself. She'd considered withholding the truth from her mother, but she wasn't sure how many lies she could keep straight. Besides, once Cheyenne heard about the bonus, Storm was sure any qualms she had would disappear. The packet of fake identification papers had arrived just after Zane had left, like Kenna said it would, and Storm wondered how much money her boss had spent to get them done—and what strings she'd had to pull to achieve it. Grateful she was alone, she'd opened the envelope and pulled out a driver's license, birth certificate, even a passport. Her face and Kenna's name and address. She was beginning to feel like she'd entered an alternate universe. "Kenna isn't here, actually. She's decided to take another trip, instead."

"But... why are you there then?"

She closed her eyes. "Because I'm taking her place."

Cheyenne's reaction was just as shrill and outraged as Storm had expected and it was some minutes before she could get her to calm down. "Listen, it's not as bad as you think."

"How can it not be?"

"Zane only wants a temporary wife." She squashed the pang of regret that coursed through her. No one had ever made her feel the way Zane did. No one had coaxed her to the edge of ecstasty three times in a single afternoon. He had to be the sexiest man she'd ever met. The most intriguing, too. She couldn't believe she'd tossed caution to the wind and made love to him—again and again and again. "It doesn't matter who he marries."

"So he knows you're not Kenna?"

Storm didn't answer.

"Oh, Storm—you're making a huge mistake," Cheyenne said.

"Kenna's paying me thirty grand." She waited a beat. Just like she'd thought, the sum silenced her mother.

"For pretending to be her for six weeks?"

"That's right. She'll get her inheritance, Zane will get his. They'll divorce in April with no one the wiser."

She could almost see the cogs turn in her mother's brain. "I guess if no one is being hurt by the deception…"

"No one's going to get hurt." Even as she said it she knew it for the lie it was. She was going to get hurt—bad. When the time came to split from Zane, she didn't know what she'd do.

"Well… do what you think is best."

Storm rolled her eyes at her mother's attempt to remove herself from any blame. "I will." She couldn't keep the edge from her voice. She was doing this to save Cheyenne's house, after all. Her mother could have sold it at any time and they'd all be far better off than they were right now. Zane wouldn't think she was Kenna, for one thing.

Of course she'd never have met him, either.

"Keep me posted. And Storm—"

"Yes?"

"Don't fall for this man, whoever he is. Remember it's a fake, and remember you don't belong in Montana. We need you back home with us when this is all over."

"Got it, Mom. 'Bye." She hung up, unable to stay on the line any longer. She didn't want to think about leaving Chance Creek. In six short weeks this would all be over and she'd take a plane back to California, leaving Zane behind forever. Of course Cheyenne wanted her to come home. She was a built in babysitter, wage-earner and housekeeper all in one. What about what she wanted, though? When would she ever stop being Cheyenne's daughter or Kenna's assistant and start her life as an independent woman? A woman free to marry a man like Zane?

She thought of the balance remaining on the cottage's mortgage.

Maybe in another twenty years.

CHAPTER FOUR

"READY TO MEET my family?" Zane asked when Storm answered the door the following morning at ten sharp. His time in the military had made him punctual among other things. Storm seemed to appreciate punctuality, too. She was dressed in a pretty, flowery skirt, a soft blouse and sandals, with a jacket over her arm and her handbag slung over her shoulder. He leaned down to steal his first kiss of the day, but frowned when Storm pulled back almost immediately. He took in the shadows under her eyes and his heart sank. Had she tossed and turned, waiting for sleep to come like he had? She looked almost—haunted. "Something wrong?"

"I... I don't think I can do this."

A wave of disappointment washed over him that had nothing to do with earning his inheritance and everything to do with wanting to be with Storm. She'd been the center of all his dreams last night—his waking as well as his sleeping fantasies. He'd counted the minutes until he could see her again. How could she think about calling anything off? "What do you mean, you can't do this?"

"This is all wrong. We're lying to everyone—lying to ourselves. It's…" She trailed off, her gaze begging him to understand. He did understand, too. It was killing him to fool the people he loved the most, but it was Heloise who'd put him in this position. You couldn't put a deadline on love, but that's exactly what she'd done.

"Look," he said, pushing past her into the room and shutting the door behind him. He dropped his hat on her bed and ran a hand over his close-cropped hair. "I get it. Maybe yesterday we went too far, too fast." He didn't think that at all, though. He thought their time together had been perfect and the idea that she might regret being with him nearly slayed him. "We'll back things off and take it slow, but we can't put off you coming home with me."

"I don't think I can keep the story straight for six weeks."

Zane cocked his head. Before he'd met Kenna, he wouldn't have pegged her as a stickler for the truth. She'd come across so mercenary in her e-mails. It was the one thing that had assured him this could work. But yesterday he'd discovered everything he'd assumed about Kenna was wrong, down to her appearance. She barely looked like that old photograph she'd sent him. It was taken at a distance too far to reconcile individual features, but even the shape of her face seemed different.

"It's just so long to pretend," she went on. "I'll be

on pins and needles the whole time."

"It's the length of time you're worried about? Not the marriage itself?" He felt a spurt of hope.

She nodded. "You signed the pre-nup already. I trust that you'll follow the plan. I know you're in this for your inheritance, not for some other nefarious reason." She smiled lopsidedly and he could tell she was trying to bolster her own courage.

He laced his hands behind his neck, searching for a way to put her mind at ease. One thing he knew for sure—he didn't want to lose her now. Not just because he needed her to secure his inheritance, but because she entranced him like no other woman he'd ever met. He needed the chance to get to know her better to see if there could be something more between them than a fake relationship—to see if she could renew his belief in love.

He wanted her for far more than a fling.

What Gunnery Sergeant Zane Hall wants, Gunnery Sergeant Zane Hall gets.

His mouth curved in memory of one of his men shouting that out in a victory toast after he'd secured a brand new, state of the art gaming system for their base in Kandahar when the old one kept breaking down.

Damn straight. He might not be in the military anymore, but he hadn't changed. He'd locked on his target: Kenna North.

And he knew exactly how to secure her.

"We won't wait six weeks to be married," he said, taking her hands in his. "We'll do it today—right now—but we won't tell anyone. We'll go back to the ranch afterwards as planned and do our best to stick out the remainder of the time until the real wedding. If at any point you think you can't take it anymore, you'll leave. We'll make up an emergency and once you're gone I'll reveal to my family that it doesn't matter—we already eloped."

"Your aunt will accept that?"

"She'll have to, but we'll hope it doesn't come to that, right?" he bluffed. In truth, Heloise would do no such thing, so he'd have to make damn sure Storm stayed. "Haven't you always wanted to spend six weeks on a ranch with a handsome Marine?" He struck a body-builder's pose, trying to lighten the mood.

Storm's mouth twitched. "You got me there. What girl wouldn't want a big country wedding to the stranger of her dreams?" She snapped her mouth shut, as if she'd said something she hadn't meant to voice aloud. Faint color traced over her cheeks.

"The stranger of your dreams, huh?" Zane knew he should let that pass, but her wording made his spirits soar. Bingo. She wasn't nearly as immune to wanting him as she was trying to make out. Their time together yesterday had hooked her as much as it did him.

"We'd better get going. Didn't you say your family was waiting for you?"

"I'd better make a call first to see if we can see the Justice of the Peace on such short notice." He was looking forward to teasing her some more, however.

Just as soon as they were married.

STORM FIDGETED ON the hard plastic seat in the waiting room at the county court building. She wasn't sure how Zane had pulled it off, but with only a couple of phone calls he'd managed to connect with someone he'd known a long time ago and asked his help in securing an appointment for a civil marriage. Apparently they'd lucked out; a local judge was presiding over weddings today and he had room in his calendar for another appointment. Now they waited in a small antechamber as couples disappeared into a larger room and reappeared holding hands and smiling at each other. Storm wondered what all their stories were. She wondered if anyone else could possibly be as nervous as she was. She was marrying the cowboy. Kenna's cowboy. In Kenna's name. This all had to be a huge mistake, but somehow she couldn't stop what was happening. She didn't want to.

Zane had taken her hand when they sat down, and she tried to draw comfort from his strong, calloused fingers, but she was failing miserably. As the minutes ticked by she was beginning to think she might faint. All her life she'd been so law abiding. So responsible.

What was she doing?

Just when she couldn't stand it anymore—when she opened her mouth to call everything off—the receptionist spoke up.

"Zane Hall?" The woman looked over her bifocals at them. "You're up next." She pointed at the double doors to the right of her utilitarian desk.

"Ready?" Zane stood up and tugged Storm to her

feet. The butterflies in her stomach picked up speed. No, she wasn't ready. She wasn't going to do this. She couldn't marry a stranger and pledge her life to him forever. She couldn't—

Zane squeezed her hand and smiled down at her. "Come on. What do you say we go get hitched?" The gleam in his eyes provoked an answering throb deep down inside of her and her breath faltered. There was something strong and steely behind the joke, as if he meant more than his teasing words might let on. Was he saying he wanted something other than a fake marriage?

There wasn't time to figure it out.

As Zane led her into the next room, she didn't pull away, though. She couldn't if she'd tried. She wanted what that look of his promised. She wanted everything and anything the cowboy had to give her. There was no way she'd walk out on the ceremony now and give up what little time she had with Zane. She knew it was all temporary. She wouldn't fool herself by pretending that this marriage was real.

But she wished it was. God, how she wished it.

What would it be like to pledge her love to a man like Zane? To say her vows and mean them? She shivered as she remembered the way they'd been together the previous day, and desire swept through her. It would be heaven to be wed to Zane. As insane as it was to think she knew this man, or could predict what a life with him would be like, instinct told her she was right where she belonged, walking arm in arm with

Zane toward the judge who would preside over their wedding. They may have put the cart before the horse—the wedding before they fell in love—but that didn't mean a thing.

Storm sighed as they walked side by side into the large, plain room where a man in black robes bent over a desk and a middle aged woman with graying hair watched them approach. She must be losing her mind. Romantic nonsense, that's all this was. She'd watched too many movies. Read too many fairy tales. There'd be no happily ever after with Zane. She wasn't even marrying him under her real name.

The man looked up. "Are you my next victims?"

"That's right." Zane shook his hand. "Zane Hall. This is Kenna North."

Cold, hard shame pierced through her. How could she daydream about marrying Zane for real when she had lied to him right from the outset? How would he react if he knew she wasn't even Kenna—that Kenna couldn't bother to stop climbing mountains long enough to marry him in person and had sent a proxy in her place?

Zane would be furious, she was sure of that.

"Marriage license?"

Zane handed it over as Storm began to tremble with the enormity of what she was doing. It wasn't just Zane's anger she had to fear if this was a criminal act, marrying under a false name. The judge made a notation on a piece of paper. "Identification?"

Storm fumbled to get the catch on her bag open,

her fingers slick with sweat, and for a minute she thought she'd left the fake driver's license behind in the motel room. Panicking, she opened her bag wider and let out the breath she'd been holding when her hand closed around it. Why was she so relieved, she wondered as the judge copied her information onto his paperwork? Was it because she hadn't been exposed as a liar? Or because her marriage to Zane—as false as it was—would go on?

When the Judge handed her license back, she shoved it far down in her bag saying a prayer of thanks that she wasn't being hauled off to jail—yet. Zane tugged her hand until she looked up at him. He leaned in close. "I agree with you," he said in a low voice.

"About what?" she whispered back. Had he read her mind? Did he think she was a criminal?

"I only want to do this once."

Another chill tingled down her spine, but this was altogether different from the guilty emotions that had almost overwhelmed her. "Only want to do what once?"

"Get married." He pulled her close and brushed a kiss over her forehead. "What do you say, Storm? Should we make this real?"

His words were so soft she wondered if she'd heard right, but he'd spoken them with enough conviction her knees went weak. Real? What did he mean, real?

"All right, let's get started," the judge said.

ZANE COULD FEEL Storm trembling and he squeezed

her hand, willing her courage as the judge took his place in front of them. He instinctively knew that if Storm quailed now, he'd lose her for good, and he didn't want to lose her. He'd never felt such a visceral reaction to a woman—never wanted anyone half so much. He couldn't let her back out now. Wouldn't let her back out ever. Storm was the one for him. He didn't know how, didn't know why, didn't even know how he could know such a thing, but he did. Storm would be his and he'd never let her go again. She stared back at him, lips parted, eyes wide, and he knew his last words had shocked her. He didn't care. He wasn't going to back down no matter how shocked she was.

"I'm Greg Masters, Justice of the Peace," the man in front of them said. "This is Susan Wright. She'll act as witness." The judge gestured to the middle-aged woman who stood beside him. He looked them over, satisfied himself that they were paying attention and shuffled the papers on the lectern in front of him. "Did you bring your own vows or do you want the standard ones?"

"Standard ones," Zane said curtly, wanting the man to get on with it before Storm balked and ran. He knew he was pressing his luck, but *what Gunnery Sergeant Zane Hall wants, Gunnery Sergeant Zane Hall gets.* Right?

He sure as hell hoped so.

"Very well. Welcome, Zane Hall. Welcome, Kenna North. Please join hands."

Zane lifted the hand he was already holding, conscious that his palm was sweaty. But so was Storm's.

She hadn't pulled away, though. A smile quirked his lips as a vision from the previous afternoon flashed through his mind. Storm on the motel room bed, her hair streaming over the coverlet, her skin flushed with desire—

What Gunnery Sergeant Zane Hall wants, Gunnery Sergeant Zane Hall gets indeed. He squeezed Storm's hand again, making a silent pledge right then and there. He would do anything—anything—to make this woman happy. He'd give his all to make their life together as successful as his parent's marriage had been. He'd work from before dawn to after dusk to provide for her and any children they might have. He'd keep her safe. He'd make her the center of his world.

Please, he prayed silently, as doubts pierced his bravado. *Please let her go through with the ceremony.*

He didn't think he could stand it if Storm ran out on him now.

WHAT DID ZANE mean, *Should we make this real?* Did he feel the same way she did? Was she drunk on a cocktail of giddiness and hope? Or did he mean he wanted her to act the part well so that they'd fool the judge and his witness? Storm couldn't tell.

Zane's grip on her fingers was nearly crushing them. One thing was clear; he wouldn't let her run now. She didn't want to run, anyway. She wanted to marry Zane.

"Zane Hall, do you take Kenna North to be your wife?" the judge said, making her suck in a sharp breath. She hadn't realized they'd plunge straight into the vows like this. Wasn't there some kind of preamble? Apparently not. As she scrambled to catch up, her heart pounding in her chest, the man went on. "Do you promise to love, honor, cherish, and protect her, forsaking all others, and holding only unto her?"

Zane turned to face her and took her other hand, as well. "I do," he said and his touch sent a shock-wave through her veins. If he was acting, he was a master at it. She couldn't turn away from the raw want visible on his face.

"Kenna North, do you take Zane Hall to be your husband? Do you promise to love, honor, cherish, and protect him, forsaking all others, and holding only unto him?"

Zane squeezed her hands, sending a pulse of desire rippling through her and she gave up any pretense that she didn't want this with all her heart. Gazing back at him, struggling to form the words, she hesitated only at the name in which she had to make this vow. She didn't want to pledge her future in Kenna's name. She wanted to do it in her own.

She couldn't, though. She couldn't keep the judge and Zane waiting any longer, either. Zane held her gaze, as if willing her to speak the answer he wanted to hear.

"I do," she said breathlessly, realizing Zane's hands were trembling as much as hers were. She blinked as a sudden emotion brought wetness to her eyes. This man—this Marine—wanted to marry her as much as she wanted him.

"Do you have your rings?" Greg Masters said.

Zane fumbled in his pocket and took out a pair of plain bands, never taking his eyes off of her.

Masters spoke again. "Zane Hall, please repeat after me."

"I, Zane Hall, take thee, Kenna North, to be my wife," Zane repeated, his voice low but strong, his intent clear in his eyes, "to have and to hold, in sickness and health, for richer or poorer, and I promise my love to you. With this ring, I thee wed."

Zane slid the thin band on Storm's finger and she sucked in an unsteady breath.

"Kenna North, repeat after me."

Storm winced again at Kenna's name, but her voice was as clear as Zane's as she repeated her vows. "I, Kenna North, take thee, Zane Hall, to be my husband—to have and to hold, in sickness and health, for richer or poorer, and I promise my love to you. With this ring, I thee wed." As she slid the ring on his fingers, she wondered what her own gaze revealed to him. Anxiety? Uncertainty?

Hope?

Masters faced them. "Zane Hall and Kenna North, in so much as the two of you have agreed to live together in matrimony, and have promised your love for each other by these vows and the exchange of your wedding rings, and by the authority vested in me by the State of Montana, I now declare you to be husband and wife." He beamed at them. "You may now kiss the bride."

STILL REELING FROM what he'd thought he'd seen in Storm's eyes, Zane pulled her roughly into a tight embrace, needing her to know that he had hope, too. He kissed her passionately, pouring his emotions into that connection. She had to understand how he felt. She had to know he'd meant every word he'd said. "It will be okay," he whispered fiercely into her ear and kissed her again. "I promise."

When he brushed her cheeks with his lips he found them wet with tears. He didn't know what that meant. All he did know was that he wanted to protect Storm from sadness. He wanted to protect her from everything.

He wanted a shot at forever with her.

STORM WIPED HER face with the back of her hand and signed on the line where the Judge pointed. A few minutes later she was back in Zane's truck headed out of town on a road that wound south. She hadn't expected to cry at the ceremony.

"You okay?" Zane asked after several minutes.

She nodded, but the truth was she didn't know if she was. Emotions assailed her that she seemed to have no control over. When Zane kissed her, she'd expected to feel happiness, or at least relief that they'd made it through the ceremony. Instead, her heart had throbbed with a bittersweet pain that pierced her to the quick.

In one quick flash she'd realized all she'd given up in her eight-year-long rush to help Cheyenne pay the bills and raise her sisters. It became all too clear what an anchor her responsibilities would be for years to come. She wanted this so badly—she wanted Zane so badly—but she couldn't have him or the life he represented. She was stuck with her family on a sinking ship with no way to ever reach land.

She'd been fooling herself if she thought this break from her family would help her see her way clearly to a solution. She'd found clarity, but of an all too different type.

She was doomed to a lifetime of servitude if she kept on her present course. How could she break free without hurting her mother and sisters, though? It had been bad enough before she met Zane, but now she understood exactly what she'd be missing during her life unless she left them. She'd never have a partner like Zane. She'd never have time for one, and even if she did, she couldn't ask any man to shackle himself to the mortgage on Cheyenne's house.

Her marriage to Zane represented everything she'd ever hoped for—except it was all fake. How cruel it was to be forced to play a role in the very life she'd always wanted. On top of that she had to masquerade as Kenna. Could thirty grand possibly be enough compensation for this nightmare? She glanced at Zane again. Yes. Anything was worth the chance to spend even six weeks with the Marine.

"Remember, as far as my brothers and their wives know, we're just engaged. In fact…" He slowed down and pulled over to the side of the road. "We'd better get these rings off before I forget." He tugged his off and held out a hand. Storm bent to pull hers off as well, distressed to have to part with it. Even if the ring didn't symbolize a real marriage, it meant so much to be even temporarily joined with Zane. She hated to give it up.

Zane closed his fingers around the two bands. "Look, I know this isn't easy. I don't know about you, but…" He gazed out the windshield at a Ram pickup loaded with hay trundling toward them. "I'm glad fate threw us together. The circumstances could be better, maybe, but at least we're here, together." He shrugged. "I'm proud to introduce you as my fiancée."

She struggled for composure. "Really? Why?"

"Are you kidding?" His smile stretched into a grin. "You're beautiful, intelligent, and you've climbed Mt. Everest. Bet none of the other women in town can match that."

Storm's spirits, newly revived, spiraled down again. She hadn't climbed Mt. Everest. She hadn't climbed much of anything. What Zane knew about her was as fake as the driver's license that proclaimed her to be Kenna. Did Zane even care for her? Or had he fallen for a lie?

Zane leaned closer. "Let's make a deal right now."

"What kind of deal?"

"That even if we only have six weeks together, they'll be the best of our lives. If we can do that, the rest will take care of itself."

When he snared her in his hazel-eyed stare, she couldn't deny him, no matter what her fears were prompting her to do. "Okay," she promised, ignoring the instincts that told her she'd regret it. "Best six weeks of our lives."

"First things first," he said, putting the truck in gear again and easing back out onto the road. "I'll teach you to ride a horse. Bet you don't know how to do that."

"No, I don't," she confirmed.

"See? We're having fun already," he said. "The six weeks will go so fast you'll blink and they'll be over. We'll top it off with a cowboy wedding and—" He cut off abruptly.

You'll blink and they'll be over. Storm nodded in agreement with his plan, but she wanted to cry all over again.

CHAPTER FIVE

"**T**HERE IT IS," Zane said as Crescent Hall came into view. Perched on a rise of ground, the tall, gray, gothic house looked every bit the foreboding mansion, but to him it had always been his definition of home. Satisfaction welled through him that this time he was here to stay.

"You left the Marines recently, right? Are you glad to be back?" Storm asked. He was happy to see she'd perked up some during their trip from town. The wedding seemed to overwhelm her and he didn't know if she'd bought into his *deal* or not. He hoped she could come around to seeing things his way. She had to if he was going to convince her to become his wife for real.

He nodded, his gaze still on his home. "You don't know the half of it." When they pulled up in front of the Hall, he got out and grabbed her luggage. "Come on. Let's meet everyone and get you settled in."

"There you are! Finally!" he heard Mason exclaim as they walked up the porch steps. The front door swung open and his brothers and their wives spilled out. A moment later he and Storm were surrounded by his family. He made the introductions, hoping Storm wasn't overwhelmed all over again. "I thought you said you were picking up Kenna and bringing her right home," Mason went on. "Got a little distracted, huh?"

Zane ignored Mason's ribbing, knowing Storm wouldn't appreciate that kind of teasing right now. "Storm, meet my oldest brother, Mason. He's the one who used to be a Navy SEAL. Mason this is Kenna North, who prefers to go by her nickname, Storm."

Mason shook her hand. "It's good to meet you, Storm. This is my wife, Regan."

Regan embraced Storm. "I'm so glad to meet you! Your wedding planner called, by the way. Mia Matheson? I've got her number for you." Regan was a petite woman with light brown hair, her belly just beginning to swell with her first pregnancy.

"Oh... thanks. I'll call her back in a day or two when I'm settled in."

"I'm Austin." Austin shook Storm's hand when Regan released her.

Zane relaxed a little. So far, so good.

"Look at you two. You're practically identical," Storm said, glancing from Austin to Zane. "Do people get confused?"

Austin chuckled. "We used to fool people all the time."

"You'd better not try to fool Storm," the woman by his side said teasingly. "Hi, I'm Ella."

Storm's eyes widened. "Ella Scales?" Zane hadn't recognized the actress when he'd first met her, but

Storm was evidently more of a movie buff. Ella was pregnant, too, but not showing yet.

"Ella Hall now." Ella smiled. "I'm done with Hollywood. I'm glad there's another California girl in town, though."

"Austin served in the Special Forces," Zane added. "But he's retired, too."

"And you all planned to retire this year—before you knew about the ranch?" Storm asked.

"Pretty much," he told her, grateful for the way she'd taken on her new role. No one looking at her would think she'd only met him the day before—or that she'd just been crying at her own wedding. "Of course Colt doesn't ever plan to retire."

"We'll see about that," Mason said and Zane knew he was thinking about Richard, the boy they'd discovered recently was Colt's son. How would his younger brother deal with finding out he was a father? Zane wasn't sure. Colt was a hard one to pin down.

"Let's get Storm inside so she can relax," Regan said, leading the way.

"Go on and get Storm settled in. We'll meet up again at lunch," Mason said. "Come down when you're ready."

Zane led the way up the steep stairs to the second floor and then down the central hallway to the large bedroom he'd stayed in since he got home. It was a comfortable room with two tall windows overlooking the yard, one door that led to a closet and another to a bathroom. A large dresser stood between the windows, and an easy chair and a queen-sized bed rounded out the furniture.

He crossed to the window to show her the view, but when he turned back to gesture her over, he realized Storm's attention had been arrested by the bed. If her expression was anything to go by, they'd just hit another snag.

He came to stand by her. "What's wrong?" Personally, he couldn't wait for night to fall so they could climb between the sheets.

"Nothing. Just—"

"After yesterday I didn't think you'd mind that we're sharing a room, or a bed. I thought you'd realized—"

"Of course. I mean, I should have. It makes sense. It's just—I can't get too attached to you."

He pulled back. "Why not?"

"This is temporary, right? That was the agreement."

Zane stared at her in shock. "The original agreement. I thought after yesterday—" He cut off and turned away. Storm touched his arm.

"I know what you mean. I feel it too, Zane, but—"

"Then stop talking about temporary." He turned to face her, crossed his arms and smiled a sudden, wicked smile. I give you my word I won't touch you—unless you want me to."

UNLESS SHE WANTED him to? She rolled her eyes at his knowing grin. Of course she wanted him to. Hadn't she made it loud and clear yesterday how much she was attracted to him?

"What are you thinking about?" He moved nearer. This close, Storm had to lift her chin to meet his gaze.

"Nothing," she said.

"I don't buy that. I think you're thinking about *this.*"

As he bent to kiss her, Storm found herself rising on tip-toe to meet him. His mouth on hers had her whole body straining toward him. She rested her hands on his chest and felt his heart beating. As he tugged her closer, she allowed herself to settle against him, aware and appreciative of every hard contour of his body.

"Well?" he asked when he finally pulled away.

"Well, what?"

"What do you think?"

"About you?"

"About all of it. Think we can have some fun to-gether these next few weeks?"

A wave of heat washed over her. Heck, yeah, she thought they could have fun together. Maybe he was right; maybe she should focus on today and to hell with tomorrow. She should view this interlude with him as time out of time—a chance to live the life she'd never get to live in the real world. She met his gaze, searching for reassurance. Could she trust this man if she took that path? She thought she could. "Yes, I bet we can."

"Good." He bent to kiss her again.

CHAPTER SIX

ANYONE WATCHING THEM would think they'd been in love for years, Zane thought later as he led her through the rest of the house. He kept a hand on her throughout the tour as they climbed up to the third floor where the old servant's quarters had been and back down to the main floor where there was a large kitchen, a formal dining room, a living room, and an office that Mason had taken over. He liked touching her, he realized. Guiding her through a doorway. Taking her elbow. Putting a hand on her waist. He wanted to belong to Storm like this. He couldn't wait until they went to bed tonight.

When they stepped out of the Hall's back door into the yard, Storm looked vastly out of place in her skirt and strappy sandals, though. It was late September and a fresh autumn breeze swooped down from the distant mountains, flooding his heart with old memories of past autumns when he was a child and his father was still alive. He could see Aaron walking back from the barn at dinner time, all four boys rushing out of the house to dogpile on him in an impromptu wrestling match. They'd been so young then—four, five and six, maybe. So full of fun. So ignorant of the hard times to come.

Storm shivered even though she wore her jacket, and he came back to the present.

"Are you cold?"

"Yes. I guess I should have brought something heavier."

"Here." He shucked off the jacket he'd thrown on and placed it around her shoulders. After a moment's hesitation she threaded her arms through the sleeves and pulled it tight around her. Its rough material clashed with her skirt, but she still looked heartbreakingly beautiful in it.

"Thanks. I'll need to buy a few extra things, I guess."

"I'll take you into town soon for a shopping trip. How about right now we go see the cattle?"

What would his father have thought of his marriage to Storm? Aaron wouldn't have liked the lie it was based on, that was for sure. What would he have counseled Zane to do about it?

"Meet the situation honorably," he could almost hear his father say. "You pledged to love her, so do your best to do just that. Be willing to be true to your vows. Let time take care of the rest."

Storm kept quiet as they walked and Zane didn't try to force a conversation. Instead, he tried to plan a course of action for the weeks ahead of them. He would honor his vows and he would definitely stay open to all possibilities, including the one in which Storm would stay when her six weeks were up. Meanwhile, there were all sorts of things they could do in between his chores—even things that didn't involve making love. Horse-back riding, for example. Camp-fires, hikes, heck, even a little mountain climbing if she felt like it.

As they approached the wire fence that surrounded the closest pasture, the nearest steer ambled over to check them out.

"He's wondering if we have any food."

"Are you sure he isn't wondering if we *are* food?" Storm held back, looking alarmed.

Zane chuckled. "Nah. If he was a bull, we might want to keep our distance, but this big boy's as gentle as a lamb." He reached out and patted the beast's neck a time or two.

Storm still held back. "I didn't realize they were so big."

"They're bred to be big."

"So people can eat them."

"That's right," Zane said carefully. "This is a cattle ranch. We raise beef here."

Storm put a hand out tentatively and touched the steer's neck with her fingertips. After a moment, she smoothed her hand down its hide. "Hello, beastie."

The steer shook its head and she pulled back.

"It makes me sad to know he'll die," she said. "I don't think I've ever met my food before."

"It's sad that anything has to die," Zane said softly.

"But that's the way this world goes. We don't slaughter the animals here. You'll never have to see it. What we do is keep them well fed and well-tended through their lives."

"And then you cut those lives short."

"I'm not going to apologize for what I do, Storm. This is me. This is who I am."

She pulled his jacket more tightly around her shoulders as if she was still cold, and Zane got a glimpse of how all this must seem to a California girl. Alien. Ugly, even.

He didn't like that characterization of his life.

"Let's go back to the Hall." Maybe they'd find Regan there. Regan was a vegetarian, and somehow she'd made peace with the family business.

"What's that way?" Storm asked, pointing down the track.

"Chance Creek. Want to see it?"

She shrugged. Zane took that as an affirmative. He led the way, but this time he didn't take her hand. The chasm between them suddenly yawned so wide he didn't know how to bridge the gulf.

They walked on, and the quiet of the ranch washed over him. There were cattle in the pastures, and there was the buzz of machinery somewhere in the distance, but between him and the far-off Absaroka Mountains was a world of space that stretched endlessly. He relaxed, breathing in the smells of home. After his years in the military, he appreciated it all the more. There was room out here. Space in which to dream. Storm would get used to the way things worked here.

He hoped.

When they reached the Creek, it was low in its banks, but burbled along merrily. "It's a bit late in the year for swimming," he told Storm, "but if we get an Indian summer, maybe we'll get a chance for a dip." He led her to a bend where the water formed a deep pool. "In July and August it's a piece of heaven."

Storm looked at it askance.

"I guess it seems small compared to the Pacific Ocean," Zane said, suddenly seeing it from her point of view.

"It would be hard to surf in," she affirmed.

He allowed himself to chuckle. She'd regained her humor and he was glad for that. "Hungry? I'll bet it's almost time for lunch."

"Sure."

As they walked back toward the Hall, she grew silent again. Halfway back Zane stopped her. "I've got to know. Are you having second thoughts?"

"No, just…"

He waited. She was so beautiful with her hair gleaming in the sun she nearly took his breath away.

"Thinking about home," she finished lamely. "It's so different here."

"Give it time, okay?" He took her hand and began to walk again. "Crescent Hall will grow on you, I guarantee it."

CRESCENT HALL WAS already growing on her. Or

rather, a certain Marine who lived here was.

A Marine who would share her bed tonight.

As much as she tried to keep her thoughts on the straight and narrow, she kept thinking about his promise not to touch her... unless she wanted him to. She wanted him to touch her again. And kiss her. And do a lot of other things, too. The hours they'd spent making love the day before had made up the most exciting sexual experience of her life. What would they do tonight to top it?

"Tell me more about you," she said as they walked back toward the Hall.

"We've covered a lot of ground. What else do you want to know?"

"Everything."

"Everything, huh? That'll take a while." He suddenly changed direction and veered off toward a stretch of woods that edged the expansive yard around the Hall.

"Where are we going?" She had to jog to keep up with him.

"I'm going to show you something that will tell you almost everything you need to know."

Storm wondered what that could possibly be, and she was more than a little surprised when she made out what looked to be two sets of climbing bars just inside the edge of the woods. They reminded her of the monkey bars at her elementary school growing up. "What are these for?"

"This is what made me the man I am today." He pointed past the climbing equipment toward a wall constructed of wood. "It's an obstacle course," he said. "My dad built it when we were just kids. We ran this thing every day. Competed against each other, against ourselves, against him."

Storm understood suddenly. That's why there were two sets of bars. It was a double course—two people could run it at once.

"Did he want you to join the Marines?"

"No, he just wanted us to be strong. He wanted to give us something to do, too. And it came in handy when he got mad at us. 'Five times around the course!'" he mimicked in a fatherly voice. "When we were really in trouble he gave us a time to beat. A really hard time. A few times I ran it for three days straight before I got it."

"That's awful!"

"That's what gives you muscles like these," he retorted and pulled off his shirt. He posed for her. "What do you think?"

"Apart from the fact you're an astounding show-off? I don't know." She reached out and traced a finger over his bicep. "Those are pretty impressive," she admitted.

"I bet you've got some pretty impressive muscles, too." He touched her arm. "Show me."

Storm panicked and pulled away. Her muscles were adequate—after all, she'd surfed for years and she did yoga most mornings. They weren't the muscles of a seasoned mountaineer, though.

"Come on." Zane reached out again.

Storm didn't know what else to do.

She launched herself into his arms and kissed him.

WHEN STORM PULLED back, Zane took her hands, unwilling to let her go. "What was that for?"

She shrugged. "I guess you're just too sexy for your own good."

He liked that idea. "You're pretty sexy yourself."

"Oh yeah? What are you going to do about it?"

"Whatever you want me to," he confessed with a chuckle. "You're the one calling the shots here."

"Really?" She seemed pleased. "Then I want you to run the obstacle course."

"Now?" He had a better idea. He tugged her closer. Storm resisted.

"I want to see what a Marine can do."

He grinned down at her. "I'll show you what a Marine can do." He snatched a kiss and was about to do it again when the stiffness in her posture told him it was time to lighten the mood. He strode toward the monkey bars that started the course. "Tell me when to go."

Storm got into the spirit of it. "On your mark. Get set. Go!"

He leaped up to the bars and crossed them in the blink of an eye, hitting the ground running as soon as he was off of them. A few short strides brought him to the climbing wall. He leaped up, grabbed the top and swung his legs up and over. Dropping to the ground on the other side, he heard Storm say, "Wow!" Zane grinned. His plan was working. What woman could resist a man at the peak of his physical prowess?

As he ran, Storm trailed after him. The exercise felt great after his last few days of relative inactivity. He'd have to make it a practice to come out here in the mornings and start his day with a lap or two—with Storm as an appreciative audience, if not as a participant.

Although why wouldn't she be a participant? She was a mountaineer. Wouldn't she appreciate the chance to exercise and hone her skills? Dressed as she was now in a skirt and sandals, she couldn't do it today, but he'd have her try it soon.

As he burst out of the forest at the far end of the course, Storm was there to cheer him on. "Go, Zane! Whooo!" she screamed as he crossed the finish line.

"Did you like that?" he said when he caught his breath again.

"I did like that. Good job."

"How about we race tomorrow—you and me?"

Storm's expression stiffened. "I don't know…"

"Why not? You'll do fine. I'll give you a head start."

"We'll see."

Zane wondered if she didn't like the idea of competing against him. "Tell you what. Let's go through the course again. I'll show you the obstacles one by one. Tomorrow you'll feel right at home here." He didn't wait for her to answer. He led her back to the first one. "I'm sure you know how to do this."

"Yes, I know how to do that one," she agreed and

relaxed a little, just as he'd hoped. He went across the bars slowly hand over hand, jumped down again and came to give her a kiss.

"My brothers and I always thought the monkey bars were too easy. We came up with all kinds of ways to cross them, including walking on top of the bars, and crossing them using only one leg and one hand."

She smiled at that snapshot of his childhood. "That sounds like fun."

At the climbing wall, he did the same thing. He backed up, leaped up and pulled himself over the tall structure, dropped down and came to give her another kiss. "That damn wall gave us a peck of trouble until we got older. Dad's rule was if you couldn't get over it by yourself during a race, you could help each other, but you had to call a time-out until both of you were over the wall and start again at the same time from the other side. We hated doing that."

"I bet."

The tire course came next.

"Is the kissing one of the obstacles?" she asked when he approached a third time.

"I prefer to think of it as one of the rewards," he said, pressing her against a handy tree and kissing her even more thoroughly. He was becoming hot and bothered, which made it a little more difficult to perform the obstacles. It was worth it, though. Each kiss she gave him was sweeter than sweet. He liked the taste of her and the way she softened under his touch. He liked the way she leaned into him, as if hungry for all he could give her.

After the rope swing across a dry gully, he decided he needed more than a kiss. He was happy to see her come to meet him. Evidently, she was enjoying this as much as he was.

"So what's the story about this one?"

"This one?" Zane searched his memory and chuckled. "There was the time Colt was drunk and fell off the swing. He had a goose egg like this on the back of his head." He held his hands a few inches apart.

"Ouch."

"It would take a lot more than that to slow Colt down. He's relentless." Zane sobered. "Hope he's okay."

"You haven't heard from him lately?"

"I talked to him last month, but Colt's a combat controller. He gets some pretty hairy missions. He said he was going to be out of contact for a while. He's never quite given us that kind of head's up before. It's got me a little spooked."

"Sorry to hear that."

"Yeah, well, he'd be laughing at me if he saw me mooning over his fate rather than getting my ass in gear and running the course."

"So run the course."

"First things first." Zane bent to kiss her again, but this time he slid his hands up under her blouse. Storm moaned and relaxed against him. Her breath hitched when he skimmed them up and traced the undersides of her breasts with his thumbs. He did it again, pushing his fingers under her bra. She twined her arms around his neck and he slid his hands around to unclasp the silky garment. Now he was able to cup her breasts and run his thumbs over her nipples.

He took his time enjoying her, but figured he'd better get back to the course. He didn't want to go too far, too fast. He was having too much fun playing this out.

He went to hook her bra back together, but Storm pushed his hands away. She wriggled within her blouse, performing some kind of miracle under there and handed him the bra after easing her arms back through her sleeves.

He took it and tucked it into his pocket, searching her face with his gaze. She was biting her lip, but her flushed cheeks and dancing eyes told him she approved of what was happening between them. When he lifted her shirt and bent to take one nipple into his mouth, she sighed and leaned against him. He took his time enjoying her breasts before he pulled away again.

"More obstacles?" she asked.

"More obstacles," he confirmed. "Get ready. I'm going to need a lot more rewards."

When he arrived at one of the balance beams his father had constructed from large logs, he practically ran across it in his eagerness to get back to her. Every time they met up again she allowed him to take things further. He was rock hard, aching to be inside of her again. He couldn't remember when he'd last felt so good.

The salmon ladder came next and with it the opportunity to really show off his prowess.

"Watch this." He grabbed hold of the metal crossbar and popped up from one level to the next with a chin-up type movement. He knew this obstacle showed off every last one of his muscles and when he jumped down he found genuine astonishment in Storm's eyes.

"That's incredible."

"You're the one who's incredible." He couldn't stop himself. He needed more of Storm. He eased her down, spread his jacket on the ground and leaned her back on top of it. He undid her blouse, transfixed by the delicious curves of her breasts, and took first one and then the other into his mouth, laving and kissing them. Storm arched back, giving him greater access, and when a few minutes later he pushed up her skirt to reveal her silky panties, she didn't protest.

What a sight she was, stretched out for his taking. Zane got to his knees, peeled down the scrap of silk and lace, pressed a kiss to her, then began a sensuous exploration that soon had her writhing beneath him and himself so hard he was growing uncomfortable.

"Aren't you going to keep running?" Storm said finally, tugging at him until he moved upward along her body, pressing kisses at intervals wherever he found bare skin.

"I don't think I could walk a step." He took her hand and pressed it against his hardness, moaning again when she immediately caressed the length of him through his jeans.

"Is this the problem?"

"That's right. Got any advice?"

She didn't answer. Instead, she worked at the buckle of his belt, then undid the button and zipper of his jeans. When she slid them down and tugged at his boxers beneath them, Zane couldn't wait anymore. He bent to fish his wallet from his pocket, searching for one of the condoms he'd tucked inside this morning. He knew how insatiable both of them were together. She helped him sheath himself, then leaned back again.

"You sure you don't want to take this back to the Hall?" He prayed to God she didn't.

Storm shook her head. "I don't want to wait. I want you now."

Heat suffused him. She couldn't possibly want him more than he wanted her. He lowered himself until he lay along the length of her, positioned himself between her legs and found her hot and slippery with need for him. Entranced by her beauty, he pressed kisses along her collarbone, then slid inside her, taking it slow to increase her pleasure and his own. Storm let out a shaky breath, her eyes fluttering closed.

Zane stroked all the way in slowly, pulled out and pushed in again. Quickly finding his rhythm, he watched her as he moved, memorizing the lift of her chin as he pushed into her and the way she arched back as he pulled out. He lifted her hands over her head and laced his fingers through hers, stroking into her again, harder. "You know, I've got a piece of paper that says you're mine," he said. He kissed her on the neck and whispered, "My wife," into her ear.

Storm's breathing grew ragged. "My husband," she whispered back.

Zane nearly lost control. "I guess that means you can make me take you any time you want."

"Any time?" she said, lifting her hips to meet him. Zane stroked in again.

"Any time," he agreed.

"I want you right now."

"You've got me."

Storm moaned as he redoubled his efforts. Zane didn't think he could last much longer. He stroked in and out, firm and strong, filling her and pulling away until the sweet friction had her panting hard and he was barely hanging on.

"Zane—"

"I'm here. I'll always be here, Storm." He increased his pace, thrusting into her again and again, until she came, crying out with it, and he came too, bucking against her until he was spent. Falling slack alongside her, he gathered her close, promising himself that next time he'd make sure they were comfortable in bed. "Are you okay?"

She laughed. "More than okay. That was…amazing. Again."

"It sure was."

CHAPTER SEVEN

"BAD NEWS," ZANE said forty-five minutes later. They'd crept back to the Hall, slunk up the stairs to shower off and change and had just congratulated themselves on getting away with it when Mason called up the stairs for him. He'd gone down to talk to his brother. Now he was back, and he didn't look happy.

"What is it?" Storm tried to calm a stab of fear. Had someone found her out?

"Aunt Heloise wants to meet you. Right now."

She breathed a sigh of relief, but she knew meeting Heloise was no little thing. From what she'd gathered, the woman was sharp, and Storm knew she had to be prepared to answer hard questions.

As Zane pulled her close and dropped a kiss on top of her head, she had to smile, though. It wouldn't be a hardship to pretend to care for him. In fact, she wouldn't have to pretend at all. Every time they made love she felt closer to Zane. She knew that was a problem, but right now she didn't care.

As they drove to town Storm took in more of her

surroundings, enjoying the passing scenery. Most of the land they traveled through belonged to large cattle spreads, but as they approached town, the houses grew closer together. Zane took them through a business district and parked a few blocks away in front of an assisted living facility. "Don't let Heloise throw you," he said before exiting the truck.

"I won't," she promised him, taking his hand as they walked inside.

They signed in at the front desk and Zane led the way to Heloise's room. No sooner had they entered it, however, than the old woman made no bones about her desire to see Storm alone. "Get off with you, Zane. You come back in a half hour. Go get me some decent coffee. And a doughnut. The things they serve me here would stand your hair on end."

When Zane left reluctantly, Storm felt as though he'd just fed her to the lions.

"Well, look at you," Heloise said, gesturing for Storm to take a seat on one end of her couch. She was a white-haired woman in her eighties with faded blue eyes and angular features, dressed carefully in slacks and a sweater. She wasn't tall, but she had presence, Storm thought. She could see why Zane and his brothers snapped to attention when she gave an order. "A pretty little thing. You look a little peaky, though. Is Zane keeping you up all night?"

Storm eyed the older woman, thankful Zane had given her a head's up about her delight in shocking people. She bit back the urge to tell Heloise just what they'd gotten up to on the obstacle course. Give the old girl a dose of her own medicine. Instead, she said, "I am a little tired, but it's nice to meet you, Heloise."

"I hear you're from California. What exactly is it that you do?"

"I climb mountains." It was uncomfortable to put on Kenna's persona again, but she knew she'd better not slip up now.

"For a living?" Heloise pursed her lips. "Didn't know you could make money doing that."

"I get grant money to help cover costs. I sell articles about my climbs. Conduct research when I can." Storm congratulated herself on sounding just like Kenna.

"Very interesting." Heloise's tone insinuated she thought there might be something untoward about it, though.

Storm smiled tightly. "Thank you."

"And now you've come to marry my Zane. He's a good man."

Storm didn't answer. It occurred to her that despite how close they'd become over the last twenty-four hours, she really knew little about him. Her conscience throbbed. She knew far too much about him, if she was honest.

Heloise lifted her chin. "What's the story?"

"What do you mean?" Storm grew wary. Had she given away the game already? Every time Zane had brought up Heloise she had thought he'd be there to help her when they met.

"It isn't easy for four boys to find wives in the space of a single year. I know they think I'm off my rocker, but I'm not. Mason and Austin had to hustle to find their wives. What about Zane? What did he have to do?"

Storm relaxed a little. She rather liked Heloise's direct manner. "He hustled, too. Wouldn't take no for an answer."

Heloise narrowed her eyes. "That glosses over a bit, I'd say."

"Maybe." Storm decided she could give as good as she got. "I'm here now and that's what matters."

"Yes, but will you stay here?"

Storm held her breath again. Heloise was sharp, she'd give her that. Would she stay? She sure wanted to.

"What would make a mountaineer want to stay in Chance Creek?" Heloise mused aloud. "You need something to anchor you. A baby would be best, but I've already played that card with Mason and Austin. I doubt I can do more with you than remind you of your duty as a wife." Storm's eyebrows shot up, but Heloise went on before she could say anything. "You need a job. No, not just a job—you'd quit that quick enough. A business." She smiled in satisfaction. "Yes, a business. That's just the ticket. What do you think about that, Miss North?"

Storm struggled to find an answer to this surprising statement. Heloise's use of Kenna's last name was a helpful reminder, though, that she had to remember she was here as an imposter. Kenna was the one married to Zane, not her. She had to behave like a dedicated mountaineer—one who planned to leave Chance Creek immediately after Thanksgiving.

"I don't want a business," she said, even as her imagination kicked into high gear. Yes, she did; a business was exactly what she'd always wanted. Something that was all hers. A chance to create something that expressed her creativity and allowed her to help make the world a more beautiful place.

"I didn't ask you if you wanted it. I told you I was giving you one." Heloise humphed. "As daft as the rest of them, aren't you? Come on."

"Where are we going?"

"On a walk."

"FOR GOD'S SAKE, Heloise; you can't just take off like that. You, too, Storm—what were you thinking?" Zane said a half-hour later when he found them around the block in a shuttered storefront. When he'd gotten back to Heloise's apartment and both of them were missing, for one wild moment he'd thought the old woman had sent Storm packing.

"Heloise wanted to show me something." Storm shrugged as if to say, *what was I supposed to do?* Zane supposed she wasn't really to blame. Heloise was a force of nature.

"What do you think about it?" Heloise asked.

"About what? About you disappearing and making me hunt you down all over town?"

"Oh, spare me the drama. A Marine can't ask a question or two and walk a block? Just like a man. About this store. Isn't it something?"

"It's a women's clothing store." Mandy's Cowgirl Emporium had been around since he was a boy. It looked now just like it looked then—stuck in a 1950s time warp. "Who wears this stuff?" The store had a musty smell and he didn't see a clerk anywhere. He couldn't blame them for wanting to hide if this was their merchandise.

"No one. The store's been closed for three months. I bought it from Amanda Hathaway when she retired. Thought it might come in handy."

He pulled a suede skirt with matching vest off a rack, both fringed to within an inch of their lives. "You thought this might come in handy?"

"Not that, idiot. The store."

Heloise's sharp tone almost made him laugh. He liked riling the old girl, but today wasn't a good time for jokes. "Handy for what?"

"For me," Storm said. "Heloise is ordering me to open it back up."

Zane struggled to keep from snapping at his aunt. He and Storm were doing so well; if she messed it up by ordering Storm around... "You can't make her do things."

"Who says I can't?" Heloise shot him an angry look and he cursed himself. She was right; she still held the deed to the ranch. She could order any of them around. "The way I see it, the women in this town need somewhere to shop. Kenna's got style. She's the one to do it."

"Kenna prefers to be called Storm," he said severely. "And she has to leave right after Thanksgiving for another trip. How is she supposed to run a store?"

"That's what managers are for." Heloise folded her arms over her chest.

He'd seen that look before. He might as well try to make Chance Creek flow backward as change her mind. If Storm didn't bow to her wishes, they might all be in trouble.

"It's okay," Storm said, as if anticipating his next words. "It's a challenge. I'll do what I can to spiff the place up. Heloise has been forewarned about my travel plans. She can't blame me if the store gets in trouble while I'm gone." She fixed a smile on Heloise. "Maybe you should be my manager. What do you say, Heloise?"

"I say I'm too old for that nonsense." But Heloise was smiling. Zane knew she secretly liked it when people showed they had backbone.

To a point.

"Are you sure that's what you want? To work in town?" he asked Storm.

"It might be interesting."

Despite himself, something eased in Zane's heart. Heloise had obviously taken a shine to Storm. And she was giving Storm a reason to stay and put down roots in Chance Creek, as inappropriate as a store was for a mountain climber. Did Storm realize how she was being manipulated? Why was she allowing it to happen?

And why had Heloise decided Storm needed manipulating? Did she really just need someone to unload the store on? Or did she want him to succeed in staying married? Heloise was tricky—he was afraid there was a catch.

Some of what he was thinking must have shown on his face, because Heloise said, "Can't an old woman do someone a good turn or two without being suspected? You two have worn me out. Take me home."

"HELOISE MUST HAVE really taken a shine to you, if she's trying to keep you here," Zane said as they walked back to his truck a half-hour later.

"I guess." Storm had to admit she was pleased with the idea of turning around a retail store. It was the kind of adventure she'd always hoped for. The kind that had seemed forever out of reach.

"If you're going to stick around, you'll need some warmer clothes," Zane said. "Better shoes, too," he added, pointing one booted foot toward the sandals she still wore.

Storm cautiously held up the key Heloise had given her. "I can take what I want from Mandy's Emporium. Let's go back and take a look."

Zane shuddered. "There's got to be a better choice."

She had to laugh at his expression. "I should at least be able to find a few more pairs of jeans and sweaters."

As it turned out, she found more than that and

soon she'd bagged up several pairs of skinny jeans which Zane declared must have been around since the last time they were in style in the 1980s, a few simple T-shirts and button downs, two A-line skirts made from fall-weight fabric, and three sweaters.

"Grab a pair of boots while you're at it," Zane suggested. "They'll hold up better on the ranch than your sandals. Here—try these. I remember Mom saying Mandy did know her footwear."

She took the boots gingerly. Cowboy boots weren't her thing, but then neither were jeans, and she had to admit they were kind of cute. "Wrong size," she said. They searched together for several minutes, neither of them talking, until they found the extra boxes in the back room. "Here. Size six." She opened the box right there and tried them on.

"Those look good." The compliment lifted her spirits. They did look good. In fact, they made her legs look a mile long. Storm grinned, and pulled them off again.

"How about some of these?" Zane had found the lingerie section of the store, such as it was. He held up a thong.

"I'll stick to what I've got back at the ranch, thank you very much." When they reached the front of the store, she hesitated. "It feels weird just walking out with this stuff. Shouldn't I leave money or something?"

"To pay yourself? If it's your store, I think you get to take whatever you want."

If it's your store.

Was it her store? Was Zane her husband? Did she belong here at all?

Or was this all a fleeting dream that would disappear in six short weeks?

CHAPTER EIGHT

"THERE HE IS, the man of the hour," Mason said, coming into the stables just before dinner. Austin followed close behind and they both clapped Zane on the back. "You sure found yourself a pretty woman. Sweet, too. Regan likes what she's seen of her so far."

"How'd you meet her, anyway?" Austin asked. "Is she really a mountain climber? She looks like a wisp of a thing to me."

Zane realized he and Storm hadn't discussed what story they'd tell the others, but he wasn't too worried. After all, Mason was the first of them to place a wife-wanted ad on the Internet and he and Regan had met online. Austin and Ella had met that way, too.

"She answered an ad," he said.

"The one I put out for you?" Mason asked as he got to work.

"No, a different one." A much more matter-of-fact and mercenary one, but he wouldn't tell his brother that.

"How long have you dated?"

"Probably not as long as we should have," Zane hedged, "but she's the one for me."

"Sometimes you just know," Mason agreed.

"Mia's called about wedding preparations a few times in the last couple of weeks," Austin said. "Have you spoken with her?"

"Not yet. Storm's taking care of that."

"Couldn't help noticing Storm's not wearing a ring," Mason said nonchalantly. At his brothers' perplexed looks he threw up his hands and admitted, "All right, it was Regan who noticed. What gives?"

"I wanted to pick it out here in town," Zane said, scrambling for a suitable answer. "I'll take Storm to get it this week."

"I'm surprised Heloise didn't give you heck about it."

"She was too busy forcing Storm to take over Mandy's Emporium. Remember that place?" He filled them in on the details, including the way Storm had tweaked Heloise with her offer of the manager position.

"She's a keeper, that's for sure," Austin said. "Maybe it's a good thing, though. When you two start your family, she won't want to keep traipsing off for months at a time to the far corners of the earth, will she?"

Zane didn't know how to answer that.

"You have discussed kids, haven't you?" his twin pressed.

"Not exactly. I mean, she wants a family. Someday." He could hear how lame he sounded. Wouldn't a couple getting married for real talk about all of this stuff? He hadn't thought to ask her.

Because they were supposed to be divorced before it ever came up.

The thought left him feeling bleak, so he was glad when Austin continued. "Better start talking about it. I know Ella and Regan are going to start in on her soon. You know how it is. Pregnancy is contagious."

"Is that how it works?" Mason said. "I always thought it had something to do with birds and bees."

Zane tuned out their jokes. The idea of having a child with Storm had taken hold of him, and he wondered what she really thought about children and family. Would she want to keep climbing mountains forever, or would she someday settle down?

"I'm glad everything turned out all right for you," Austin said, breaking into his thoughts. "Whether or not you have kids, I'm sure you both will be very happy."

Suddenly Zane wasn't sure about that at all. It hit him hard how little time he had to convince Storm to stay with him. Just under six weeks. He'd better get started now.

"DETAILS. WE NEED details," Regan said when Storm ventured downstairs again and found the two women alone in the kitchen, preparing for supper.

"We want the whole story about how you two met," Ella said. She poured Storm a cup of coffee and beckoned her to take a seat at the small kitchen table. A large, solid, shaggy black dog sat underneath it. Ella tracked the direction of her glance. "That's Milo. Friendliest mutt you've ever met."

"Hi Milo," Storm said, buying time. She perched on the edge of the seat, blowing on her coffee. "What about you two? How did you meet Mason and Austin?"

Regan laughed and colored a little. "I actually met Mason because of mixing social media with alcohol. I saw his online ad one night when I was alone and wasted, thought it was hilarious, and wrote him an e-mail straight out of a Jane Austen movie. He wrote back and the next thing I knew we were Skyping and calling and emailing back and forth. He wouldn't give up no matter how I tried to break things off. I mean, it was crazy, right? Meeting someone online like that. But it was romantic, too, and I fell in love with him—even before I ever met him in person. It was like we were meant to be together. When I came here I fell in love with Crescent Hall, too. Mason and I got married and the rest is history."

"My story is even crazier than Regan's," Ella said, setting the table. "I had just gotten back on my feet after the disaster at the Oscars."

Storm nodded. She watched enough television to know what Ella meant. Ella had been a candidate for the Best Supporting Actress award but another actress, Kaylee Lipenhauer, won and stole Ella's fiancée from her all in one blow by announcing on stage that she'd been having an affair with Anthony Black for months and was pregnant with his child. The scandal had rocked Hollywood, and Ella had disappeared for months, only to return on an episode of Morning with Myra. But that hadn't gone well, either. The host, Myra Cramer, set her up by inviting Anthony and Kaylee on the show, too.

"You clocked Anthony," Storm said. "I thought he deserved it."

Ella went to get glasses from a cabinet. "He did deserve it, but my career was tanking and I needed somewhere to hide. Austin put up a different wife-wanted ad saying he wanted a pretend wife for about a year. It looked like the perfect answer to my problems."

"So you're just pretending to be Austin's wife?" Storm felt a rush of relief. She would be able to confess everything to them. They'd understand what she was going through and help her figure out what to do.

"Only briefly. The minute I met Austin in person I fell for him. We had some issues to work through, but soon enough it was clear our marriage would be real. We had a vow renewal ceremony that was really our true wedding. So in the end it all worked out for the best." Ella's smile was radiant.

The women turned to her expectantly, and Storm's heart sank. She couldn't confess after all—couldn't admit that she and Zane were together only temporarily. She'd have to craft her story carefully.

"Zane posted a wife-wanted ad, too," she began.

ZANE COULDN'T KEEP his eyes off his watch as he

finished up his evening chores after dinner that night. How soon could he wrest Storm away from the others and get her upstairs? He couldn't wait to be alone together with her again, and the thought of the bed they'd share tonight had his mind racing with all kinds of interesting possibilities.

When he came back inside, he heard the other couples chatting in the living room and the sound of a football game on the television. Storm was in the kitchen by herself, pouring a drink of water from the tap.

He came up behind her and wrapped his arms around her waist. "Missed you," he murmured into her neck, pressing a kiss under her ear.

"You weren't gone that long."

"Long enough." He pressed his hips against her bottom, knowing she'd feel the evidence of his interest. "Come on. Let's sneak away before they hear us."

They gained the stairs without being discovered and by the time they reached the bedroom, they were laughing like teenagers.

"You watch. Someone will call us just as we get to the good part." Zane groaned as Storm wrapped her arms around his neck and pulled him down for a deep kiss.

"We'll just have to be fast then."

"How fast?" The thought of a quickie turned him on. Although he hoped it would be followed by a long, slow session of lovemaking. If he knew Storm better he'd put some moves on her that would knock her socks off, but he didn't want to risk scaring her away.

She moved to lock the door. "I doubt you can be fast enough to suit me. You men are all alike with your need for long, drawn-out foreplay." She peeped at him mischievously over her shoulder.

So much for worrying about scaring her. Zane tugged her back to him, spun her around, bent her over the bed and yanked her skirt up to expose her bottom. He hooked his thumbs in the band of her panties. "This fast enough?"

"So far, so good, but you're a little overdressed, sailor." Storm was laughing, but as he slipped them off, parted her legs and unbuckled his belt, her breathing went ragged.

Zane's wasn't any steadier. He was taken aback by how right this felt as he shucked off his jeans and boxers. He'd only met Storm in person yesterday, but he felt like he'd known her for far longer. The fact they were married only served to rev him up further. Her body enticed him and her personality intrigued him. With his hands on her, he felt like he could do no wrong. She moved so easily with him, as if anticipating what he meant to do. Right now the sight of her bent form, her skirt around her waist, her legs wide, inviting him in, snared him in bonds of want and need he knew he'd never be able to shake.

He reached for a condom from the drawer in the bedside table, slipped one on, gripped her hips, positioned himself between her legs and let himself nudge against her. She immediately pressed backward, urging him inside, needing no foreplay to be ready for him. He'd never been with a woman who made it all seem so easy. There were no hang-ups with Storm. Her needs and his matched perfectly. When Zane reached around her waist to dip a hand between her legs, and began to swirl his fingers, she moaned with pleasure.

"Is that good?"

"That's so good."

"Honey, you can't imagine how good I feel right now." He pressed into her an inch at a time, allowing both of them to anticipate what was to come. When he was fully inside her, he pulled out and pressed in again. Storm strained back against him, begging with her body for more. As he increased his pace, reveling in the sweet friction between them, her muscles began to tremble. One hand skimming up to cup a breast, the other rubbing her sex, he could feel her heart racing and her breath quickening until he knew she was close.

"Zane—"

He responded to her urgings, thrusting inside her until he pushed her over the edge of ecstasy. Her breathy cries sounded just as he grunted his release and they came together, pulses of raw pleasure pounding through his veins until Zane's head swum and he fought to keep his balance.

When it was over Storm collapsed forward, resting her elbows on the bed with her head in her hands until Zane pulled out of her and helped her up. "You are the sexiest woman alive."

She turned in his arms. "I can't believe how good

you make me feel."

"Zane? We've got company!" Mason shouted up the stairs from the floor below.

Zane chuckled. "What did I tell you?" He turned to shout back, "We'll be down in a minute."

"Now!"

Zane frowned. "Sounds like there's trouble." He kissed Storm absently, then grabbed his clothes and headed for the bathroom. By the time he came out again Storm had gathered her things and was waiting for her turn. "I'll be back in a flash," he told her.

"I'm looking forward to it."

THERE WAS NO way she could leave when her six weeks were up, Storm decided as she hurriedly cleaned up and got dressed. No one had ever made her feel like Zane did. She felt utterly unashamed with him, like she could do anything—or ask him to do anything— without a worry in the world about embarrassment. The way he made love to her told her everything she needed to know. He worshipped her body and made her want to worship his. She couldn't wait for Zane to finish up downstairs and come back for another round.

By the time she was dressed, however, Zane wasn't back. She opened the bedroom door to hear angry voices traveling up the stairwell. She padded down the hall and was halfway down the stairs when the entryway came into view.

"...bad enough you took my ranch. Now you've taken Belinda's store, too?" The man facing Zane was nearly spitting with rage as he yelled at him.

"I don't know what you're talking about, Darren." Zane didn't budge.

The man looked up, spotted Storm standing there. She sucked in a surprised breath.

"I'm talking about that bitch you brought home. I'm talking about the store that Heloise promised to Belinda!"

Storm gripped the bannister, fighting the urge to run right back upstairs.

"Don't talk about my fiancée like that." Zane surged forward, but Darren took a step back.

"I won't stand for it." He stood half on the porch, half in the doorway, his body language belying his bold words. Storm clutched the bannister, noting the resemblance between him and the Hall brothers. But where the Halls stood tall and proud with from years of military discipline, Darren's shoulders were rounded and his face pinched. "You all won't be happy until you run us into the ground. It's not right!"

"You've run yourself into the ground. You've only got yourself to blame." Austin backed up his twin. Storm was grateful she wasn't Darren. The Hall boys as a united front were fearsome to behold.

Darren stepped forward again. His steel-blue-eyed gaze caught hers and held her in place. "You tell her to keep away from Belinda's shop. You tell her to go back home where she came from."

Zane strong-armed Darren right out the door. The other men followed and the shouting became indistinct, but she could see Darren striding toward a black pickup parked askew in the drive. He climbed in, slammed his door and made a U-turn over the lawn before zooming away down the road. Her heart pounded in her chest as Mason returned inside, followed quickly by Zane and Austin. They spotted her on the stairs.

"Hell," Zane said, coming toward her. "I wish you hadn't heard all of that."

"Who was that?"

"Cousin Darren," Mason said. "Black sheep of the family."

Storm came down the rest of the steps just as Regan and Ella came in from the back of the house. "What was that all about?" Ella asked.

"Darren," Mason said again. "Maybe we'd better go sit down and have a talk. All of us." When they were seated at the dining room table, he went on. "Storm, Darren's dad took over this ranch when our father died twelve years ago, and kicked us off of it. He ran it into the ground and then started to dismantle it. The only good thing he did was probably an accident. He never changed his will. Instead of leaving the ranch to Darren, the old will he had in place since before he married left it to Heloise in the case of his passing."

"When he died, Heloise offered it to us with the conditions you know about." Zane took up the thread. "Obviously, that pissed Darren off. I've been wondering when he'd come around and start trouble. I'm sorry he picked today to do so."

Storm swallowed. "It's because of the store. Because Heloise gave it to me." She hadn't dreamed she was accepting something that belonged to someone else.

"She promised it to Belinda?" Ella asked.

"It's the first I've heard of it," Storm told her. "I'll talk to Heloise and tell her if that's the case, then I'll back off." As much as it killed her to think about doing that. She'd wanted so badly to have one thing of her own.

And she would. Someday.

Maybe.

"I bet you'll find that Heloise promised her no such thing," Austin said.

"Still, I don't want to be the cause of a family rift."

All three Hall boys chuckled. "This particular rift has gone on for ages. You're just collateral damage." Mason checked his watch. "The game's almost over. I want to catch the end. You coming?" he asked Zane.

"Nah. Storm's tired," Zane said, winking at her. "We'll see the rest of you tomorrow."

CHAPTER NINE

THE FOLLOWING MORNING, Zane slipped out early to tend to his chores, the memory of his night with Storm keeping him from noticing the chill in the air. After he'd convinced her not to worry about Darren's threats, they'd made love again, this time in bed, and he'd taken the time to explore every beautiful inch of her. Darren's accusations had left a sour taste in his mouth, however, that all those delightful memories couldn't dislodge. He'd better talk to Heloise today and sort things out. It wasn't like Storm needed a store to keep her busy, between her climbing excursions and the fact she was supposed to leave right after Thanksgiving, but he had a feeling the store could act as a tie between her and Chance Creek. Something about Mandy's Emporium had captured her interest. He couldn't help but want to capitalize on that.

He'd decided he needed to show Storm more of what life on the ranch could offer, as well, and teaching her to ride was the logical way to start. Riding was something fun they could do together, and it would give him a way to show her all the best parts of the ranch.

As for Darren… Heloise had promised that store to Storm, and her strategy had worked—Storm had liked the idea of the challenge of bringing it back to life. It made it more likely she'd stay in Chance Creek, at least until Thanksgiving. He wasn't going to let Darren ruin that.

But wasn't that what his cousin's family was put on this earth to do? He felt no pity for Darren. Zeke had turned into a right old bastard when Zane's father had died. Darren wasn't any better. Zane would never forget standing just where Storm had this afternoon on the stairs, clutching the bannister while his uncle had stolen his home away. The pain he'd felt from the betrayal was still fresh in his heart. This time he'd do whatever it took to keep his family safe, together and living on the ranch. That included Storm, too.

Zane found his hands had balled into fists. He forced himself to straighten his fingers and shake off the past. The Hall was theirs again and there was nothing Darren could do to take it away. He wasn't going to take Storm's store, either.

When his chores were over, he went back upstairs in the Hall and woke Storm with a kiss.

"Morning," she said as she stretched. She lifted her head and glanced at the clock. "You should have woken me earlier."

"You got a date?"

"I need to start work on the store," she said, sitting up. "If it really is my store. I guess I'd better start with a call to Heloise."

"Later. First things first. I'm going to teach you to ride."

"Oh, really?" She shot him an arch look. "I thought I proved last night I was pretty good at that."

"Oh, you are good. Really, really good." He kissed her until she fell over. "Another quickie?" he asked when she began to fumble with his belt.

"Quickie, slowie, whatever you've got in you, cowboy."

He showed her what he had and she seemed to appreciate it. In fact, she rolled him over, crouched above him and took him inside her mouth, teasing and tempting him with her tongue and hands until he couldn't wait to be inside of her.

He lifted her up to straddle him, then stopped with a groan and fumbled in the bedside table for a condom. "I can't wait until we don't need these anymore. I know I'm clean. What about you?"

"That's not the issue. The problem is I'm not on the pill right now." She shrugged at his quizzical expression. "I haven't had a serious boyfriend in a long time, and I have a mother who's a worry-wart about any kind of medication. Seemed silly to be on it when I didn't need it."

Zane had no idea why the thought of her not being on birth control was such a turn on. Usually it was the other way around, but then again he'd never been with a woman he loved before—not like this.

He stopped. Stared at Storm perched above him,

glorious in her nakedness. Did he love her—already? How was that even possible?

"What?" Storm asked.

"You take my breath away," he said, deciding to think about love later. "And it doesn't make a lick of sense, but I'd love to toss this condom away, too."

Her brow furrowed as if she was trying to puzzle out his meaning. "You want... a baby?" she said finally, sitting back on her haunches.

Her bottom pressed against him had him on fire all over again and he barely suppressed a groan. "With you? Hell, yeah, I do. Told you it makes no sense. I've always thought I'd be a family man, though. Now that I'm out of the service, it's on my mind."

She lifted up on her knees, took the condom from his hand, tore open the wrapper and popped it out. She sheathed him with light fingers that drove him wild, then positioned him so she could take him inside. Braced against him, sighing as she sank down on top of him, she said, "If I was going to have kids with anyone, I'd want it to be with someone like you."

He caught her wrists in his hand. "Someone like me?"

"Someone not afraid of commitment and responsibility."

"Do you want children?"

"Someday."

"How many?" He swallowed as she raised herself on her knees and sank down again. Damn, she felt good.

"I don't know. Two. Maybe three."

"How about a half-dozen?"

She laughed and the sensation of it pulsed through him. "I don't know about that."

"Even if I did this?" He began to pump into her and her expression changed into one of bliss as she moved with him, rising and falling until she was bouncing on top of him. The lift and fall of her breasts entranced him, as did her obvious pleasure. They spoke no more until Storm cried out and he came, too, crashing against her until both of them were drained and panting for breath.

She slid off of him and he pulled her close. "Is there room for me in your life for real?" he asked, wrapping his arms tight around her.

"I want there to be."

BY THE TIME Storm stumbled downstairs, Zane having gone back to his chores, breakfast was long over. Regan was writing up a shopping list and Ella folding laundry.

"There's no washer and dryer in the bunkhouse," she explained to Storm. "I guess I'm here more than I'm home some days. Besides, it's fun to have company."

Storm nodded. "What else do you two do around here?" she asked as she prepared her breakfast.

"I've been writing," Ella said and shrugged. "I don't know if anything will come of it."

"I help the men out all I can," Regan said. "When I

first arrived it was just Mason and me, and I liked the work. Now that I'm pregnant, I stay away from the more dangerous jobs, but I still like being outdoors, getting dirty and working with my hands. Ella and I split the inside chores, so there's plenty of time to do both."

"Sounds nice." But Storm wondered how she fit in. Maybe she'd spend all her time at her store—if it turned out to be her store. Zane had promised to check into that today.

She ate her breakfast swiftly, then hurried to wash up her dishes. She cast an eye over the kitchen. "Is there anything else that needs to be washed?"

"Nope, we got everything earlier."

"I'll sweep up next."

"Did that already," Regan said.

"I could check on the laundry."

"This is the last load," Ella said, laughing. "We've got a system going."

"A daily list," Regan added, pointing to a piece of paper on the refrigerator where jobs were divided between the two women.

"Let me pick a few things off of there to help you two out."

The women exchanged a glance. "You'll have to be up pretty early if you want to do that," Regan explained with a shrug. "The men get up before dawn and we've both gotten in the habit of doing most of the inside chores then."

"Okay." An awkward silence descended until Ella

said, "I know—let's talk over your wedding plans. Did you get in touch with Mia yet?"

The wedding? It took her a moment to remember that Ella and Regan didn't know she'd gotten married by the Justice of the Peace, and they expected her to be looking forward to the church affair she was supposed to be planning. She might have looked forward to it if it didn't signal the end of her time here. She still hadn't called Mia, and she didn't wish to discuss the details with Ella and Regan either.

The other women were waiting for her answer, though. "Um... I'm supposed to have a riding lesson. I'll call her afterward."

"Oh, right. Zane mentioned that. You'll find him out in the stables with the others," Regan said, nodding.

Storm escaped out the back door, and as the autumn sunshine and fresh air swept the cobwebs from her brain, she let her worries fall away. Time enough to think about the wedding later. Right now she was going to enjoy her time with Zane. She couldn't believe the way he'd brought up having children as if talking about raising a family was the most natural thing in the world. She remembered bringing up the topic of children with Todd once—and only once. He hadn't been able to hide his horror at the idea of that kind of responsibility.

Zane wasn't afraid of responsibility, though. Instead, he seemed to embrace it. Up hours before her, but cheerful when he came to wake her up, he appeared to relish the chores that faced him on the ranch.

He obviously liked the idea of being a father, too. Zane would make an incredibly sexy father.

Too bad she wouldn't get to see it, she reminded herself. She couldn't get caught up in thinking about the future, when the future she was dreaming about didn't belong to her.

She found Zane leading a horse out to a corral. He gestured for her to follow him and when he'd shut the gate behind them, urged her to come closer to the horse.

"This is Jasper." He smoothed a hand down Jasper's neck. "He's very patient. You'll do fine with him."

"Hello, Jasper." Storm touched the horse hesitantly, finding it hard not to stare at Zane. Dressed in work clothes, he was every inch the cowboy today, down to his hat and boots. She wished she'd been able to see him in his uniform, but she found it hard to believe he could look any more handsome than he did right now.

"Let him smell you."

She stood as ordered while the horse snuffled a few times, evidently getting a sense of her scent. Zane coached her patiently—almost tenderly—and as the lesson proceeded, Storm relaxed. When Zane lifted her into the saddle, exhilaration swooped through her, taking her off guard. Zane led the horse around the corral in a circle and she felt wonder that such a magnificent creature would let her ride him.

"It's fun, huh?"

She shrugged. "If I'm going to live on a ranch, I

guess it's practical for me to know how to ride."

His grin told her she wasn't fooling him one bit. "Sure. And… it's fun."

She gave in. "It *is* fun."

They looped around the corral several more times before Zane opened the gate.

"What are you doing?" Storm asked in alarm.

"Taking you on a real ride." Before she could protest, he leaped up into the saddle behind her, encircled her in his arms and took the reins. Jasper seemed used to such treatment and responded to Zane's slightest cues. Soon they were trotting down the track toward Chance Creek. Storm clung to the pommel for dear life until Zane chuckled. "I won't let you fall." He snugged his thighs against hers and with his strong chest to lean against and his arms cradling her, Storm realized she was perfectly safe.

Safe from falling off the horse, anyway.

She wasn't safe from getting her heart broken, though. All the talk about the wedding had reminded Storm that she was living in a fool's paradise. It didn't matter if she fell in love with Zane or if he loved her back—at the end of the day, she'd have to leave him. His marriage was to Kenna, not to her. She had a feeling he wouldn't be too pleased when he discovered how he'd been duped.

CHAPTER TEN

Z ANE LOVED HAVING Storm in his arms like this, but she had grown tense and he wasn't sure if she was still afraid of the horse, or if something else had upset her.

"I won't let you fall," he assured her.

"I know. It's just… I'm going to miss this when I go."

Zane saw his opening. "Then don't go."

"We can't make plans for the future like that yet. We don't know each other—not really," she added when he chuckled.

"I feel like I know you better than almost anyone else I've ever met."

"Oh yeah? What's my favorite color?"

He remembered the skirt she'd worn when he'd first met her. "Green."

"Hmph. Lucky guess."

He eased the horse to a stop and leaned forward to try to see her face. "I don't want you to leave after Thanksgiving. Stay here with me. We'll get to know each other even better."

She made a face he couldn't decipher. "I have responsibilities," she said. "I can't let my climbing team down, for one thing. A lot of people depend on me."

He understood that all too well. "Then go on this next climb, but come right back afterward. And don't hurry away again anytime soon. We can figure this out."

"I don't think so," she said softly.

A chill raked down his spine. He hadn't expected that answer. "Why not?"

"Because I can't be what you want. A full-time wife. The mother to your children. That's not who I am." She seemed to struggle with that last sentence.

Zane understood. She felt torn between conflicting desires. She defined herself as a mountaineer and she didn't want to lose what must be a wonderful part of her life, but when they'd spoken of children last night there'd been a yearning in her eyes he was sure meant that motherhood was important to her, too.

He probably shouldn't have jumped the gun like he had, either. They were speeding through relationship stages like there was no tomorrow. That was Heloise's fault though. With her deadline looming over him, he felt like he had to rush things.

It was easy to talk to Storm, too. About kids, the ranch, sex...

"You don't have to choose between me and mountain climbing. I'd never ask for that."

"You say that now," she told him sadly, "but what would you feel if I got pregnant? Would you be content to let me leave for months on end when we had a newborn?"

"Would *you* be content with that?" He couldn't believe that of her. He could fully understand her not wanting to give up her career, but she wouldn't leave a newborn…

"I think you'd better take me home." Storm turned forward, and he felt the distance between them increase again.

He pressed his cheek against her hair. "We're going to find a way through this."

When she didn't answer, he reluctantly turned Jasper around.

PRETENDING TO BE Kenna was getting harder by the minute, Storm thought as she strode back toward the Hall a few minutes later. She would never leave a baby at home while she traveled for months. That wasn't her at all. Every time she was with Zane she wanted to blurt out the truth of who she really was, but she couldn't do that. She had to keep up the pretense of being Kenna. For one thing, she had no idea how he'd react when he found out what she'd done. For another, she still needed the bonus Kenna had promised her to help get her family current on its bills. Married or not, she couldn't—wouldn't—ask Zane for help with that matter. The cottage was a money trap that could suck both of them under.

It was no use asking herself why she'd gone along with her mother so long in keeping it, rather than selling the thing and getting free from the mountain of debt it represented. She knew exactly why Cheyenne clung to the house—it was her way of clinging to Mitch.

Storm had felt the same way for the first few years after her father had died. If they'd had to leave their home on top of losing him, she would have been devastated. Now she felt differently. They had lost too much in their attempt to keep it. She had never been able to afford college. Neither would her sisters.

It was time to sell.

She felt in her pocket for her phone, pulled it out and looked at it for a long minute.

No, not now. Cheyenne would be at work. She'd have to wait for tonight to call and have the talk that was long overdue. She cast about for something else to do to take her mind off her mother—and Zane. She needed a distraction.

The store.

Storm nodded. She'd go into town and spend the rest of the morning at Mandy's, if she could get a ride, but there was a phone call she needed to make first. Not to her mother—to someone else. Her short time with Zane had taught her that she didn't want to beat around the bush in relationships anymore. She wanted to speak plainly and trust others to do the same. That meant she couldn't ignore Darren's allegations. Zane obviously hadn't followed up on it yet with Heloise, so Storm thought she'd get the information she needed straight from the horse's mouth. A bit of a search on the Internet located the number for Darren. She made the call before she could change her mind and when a woman's voice answered she crossed her fingers and asked, "Is Belinda there?"

"Speaking." The woman sounded tired.

"Belinda, my name is Storm. You might have heard of me."

"Zane's bride." No change in the tone of her voice. Storm frowned. She'd expected anger—maybe even a hang up.

"That's right. I arrived Saturday, met Heloise for the first time and she offered me Mandy's old store. It sounds like that was meant for you, though."

There was a silence on the other end. "That's Darren for you. It wasn't promised to me if that's what you mean. Heloise mentioned the store to me when she bought it. I mentioned it to Darren. He thought it should be ours on account of you all getting the Hall. I guess he's half-convinced himself now it was Heloise's idea, not his."

"I can see why he might think it was fair. I wanted you to know I wasn't trying to take something that was rightfully yours."

"No, I don't expect you were. Don't worry about it." She sounded like she was about to hang up.

"Wait—wait a minute. Belinda?"

"Yeah?"

Storm couldn't let the conversation end like this. She hadn't liked the way Darren had talked to her—or to Zane—but the woman on the other end of the line sounded so defeated she couldn't stand it. She might regret this, but she thought it was possible one good thing could come of her time here in Chance Creek. Maybe she could help end the feud between the Halls that had been going on for so long. "Would you like to help me?"

"With what?" Now Belinda sounded annoyed.

"Would you like to come work for me at the store?" Storm quailed, even as she spoke. She'd never met Belinda. Didn't know the first thing about her. What if she was mean, or stole from the till, or scared away all the customers?

"Work for you? At Mandy's?" For the first time Storm heard a spark of life in the woman's voice. "I've been looking for a job, but I don't have much experience."

"You don't need any experience. Could you meet me there in twenty minutes so we can talk things through? I have a key." Storm wasn't sure how she'd get into town, but she'd work that out.

"Yes, I think I can. Yes, I'll be there. Twenty minutes." Belinda hung up and Storm had to smile. Belinda's voice had transformed in those last few sentences. Storm couldn't wait to meet the mystery woman and see just what she'd gotten herself into. At least now she had something to concentrate on other than the mess she'd made of her life so far.

Ella gladly lent her a car and Storm escaped before Zane could come looking for her again. Twenty minutes later she was struggling with the lock on the store's front door when a sharp-faced woman with a bad bleach job growing out rounded the corner and walked briskly toward her. She wore jeans and battered old cowboy boots. She carried a few extra pounds and there was a stain on the hem of her knit shirt, but the purse she carried was stylish and her makeup was expertly done.

"Are you Storm?" the woman asked.

"Yes. Belinda?" Storm smiled in greeting. "Come on in. Let's take a look around."

Belinda followed her inside, shoved her hands in her pants pockets, and said, "You're from California?"

"That's right."

"You look it."

Storm decided to take that as a compliment. "Thanks."

"I guess I look like a hick to you."

"Of course not." Storm frowned at Belinda's tone. "You look like a woman juggling a lot of balls. You have children, right?"

"Five of them."

"School age?"

"My youngest just started Kindergarten. Thank God." Belinda swallowed. "I mean, I love them and all…"

"Five is a lot." Storm chuckled. "I think you're allowed to be relieved they're in school."

"Anyway, I'd be glad to help out here—if you want me."

"I appreciate it." Storm began to walk around the

store and check out the inventory. It was as out of date and depressing as she'd remembered it being. "How long have you lived in Chance Creek?"

"All my life." Belinda laughed hollowly. "Can't seem to escape it."

"Do you want to?"

The other woman began to move around the store, too, running her hands over the items of clothing. "I don't want to leave Chance Creek so much as… well… I want something to change. Know what I mean?"

"Yes, I do." How many times had she wanted something similar back in California, but hadn't been able to put her finger on what exactly to do about it? Being in Montana was giving her a lot of perspective on her old life, especially about the way she'd let problems drag on and on without doing much to try to solve them. That was going to change. "I think we need to start by getting rid of all this stuff. I mean, is there anything good in here?"

"These aren't bad." Belinda pulled out a pair of boot cut jeans that Storm had to admit were just fine. "This too." She pulled out a plaid shirt and waved it at Storm. "I mean, you wouldn't find them on Rodeo Drive, but women in Chance Creek need clothes to garden in and clean their houses and run the kids around, you know?"

"Okay." Storm had an inspiration. "That's where you can start—separating out the good from the bad. Let's clear two racks. We'll hang things to keep on one. The other will be for things to get rid of."

"We could have an in-store garage sale," Belinda suggested.

"Great idea. We'll price everything super cheap. Maybe someone will buy them."

"Everyone will buy them—for quilt squares if nothing else."

"Quilt squares?" Storm stopped in her tracks. "Does anyone actually quilt anymore?"

Belinda turned to stare at her. "Of course. I guess they don't in California, though."

"None of my friends do." Storm shrugged, realizing with a small ache that she didn't have many friends, seeing as she was always so busy. Maybe lots of women in California quilted. What would she know about it? She pulled everything off of two wheeled racks and moved them into the center of the store, hoping Belinda hadn't noticed her distress. "Let's get started."

Time flew by as they got into the task and soon Storm's sorrow passed away and they were chatting easily, showing each other the things they found and debating the merits of various items of clothing. The sale rack filled up faster than the keeper rack, but there was more to keep than Storm had imagined. She cringed at a few of the things Belinda added to it, but mostly agreed with her choices.

"I've got to go," Belinda exclaimed several hours later. "Time to pick up Joey from Kindergarten."

"Can you come tomorrow?"

"You bet!" Belinda bit her lip. "I mean, if you want me to."

"I definitely do. You and I are going to whip this store into shape."

"I've had more fun this morning than I've had in ages," Belinda said in a burst of enthusiasm. "Thank you for this."

"Oh, your time card!" Storm ran to find a piece of paper in her purse. "Let's write down your hours for today. I'll get something more official set up soon." She named a wage that seemed awfully low, but Belinda seemed grateful for it. Storm hoped the money Heloise was giving her to cover startup costs would cover Belinda's pay, too.

"See you tomorrow!"

"See you."

Alone once more, Storm took more time to look around the store. Yes, she could definitely make something of it.

But would she be here long enough to see it come to fruition?

CHAPTER ELEVEN

"WHAT'S WRONG?" ZANE asked when he reached the northwest pasture. He'd received a call from Mason that he'd better get out there quick, and had left off saddling up his horse for a morning ride and taken one of the utility vehicles instead to save time.

Mason gestured to a break in the fencing where the wires dangled. "Just dumb luck that the cattle have been staying on the eastern end. None of them discovered the break yet, so we didn't lose any."

"Looks like that's been cut." Zane approached the fence.

"Damn straight. And you know who did it." Austin's arms were crossed over his chest.

"You think it was Darren?"

"Of course it was Darren. Who else?"

"Could be kids with too much time on their hands," Mason said.

Zane shook his head. "Darren wants to make us look bad, so Heloise will change her mind."

"He wants to damage the herd and bankrupt us,"

Austin said.

"He might want to do that, but I doubt he can figure out a way," Mason said. "He'll just do what he can to make things miserable." He glanced back at the fence. "If he even did this."

"You're underestimating Darren. It wouldn't take much to drain our profits enough to make us unable to go on. I won't ask Ella to underwrite the cattle ranch." Austin was adamant, and Zane understood his position. As a former actress, Ella had money in the bank, but Austin didn't want to risk any of it on this particular venture. It was too chancy—especially since it only took Colt reneging on his promise to get married to ruin it for all of them.

"So what do we do?" Zane calculated the time it would take to mend the fence.

"We keep our eyes open. Keep the dogs outside for a few nights to warn us of intruders." Mason came to stand beside Zane. "You make sure to keep your bride happy and your wedding on track. The last thing we need is any more ugly surprises."

STORM CAUGHT A ride into town with Ella the next day, met Belinda at the store and got to work where they'd left off the day before.

After working and chatting for an hour or so, they fell into a companionable silence for a while that allowed Storm's mind free range to think about her business.

"I want this place to be more than a clothing

store," she said after some minutes had passed.

"In what way?" Belinda kept sorting.

"I want it to be a place that's got everything a person needs to feel like they're surrounded by beauty."

"A person just needs to look out the door for that. Chance Creek's beautiful all on its own."

"How about inside your house? How about the clothes you wear? So much of what we own is just... good enough, you know what I mean? It doesn't really fit. It isn't really right. It's not all that it could be."

Belinda looked down at her clothes. "We're not all built like mannequins, for one thing. We're not made of money, either."

"I know that. I'll have to look hard to find brands of clothing and housewares to stock that are beautiful, yet functional. I'll get to know my customers because this town is so small. Maybe I can tailor my stock to the people who shop here."

"Is that possible?"

"I don't see why not," Storm mused. "I'm in a pretty sweet position because for once in my life I don't need a lot of money. I can take chances." Instantly guilt swept over her. Shouldn't she be sending every extra penny back to Cheyenne? And what about contributing to the ranch's expenses?

What about the fact she was leaving in six weeks, for that matter? She shook her head at her own fantasy. She'd have no time to tailor her stock to her customers.

"That sounds nice." Belinda kept on working. Now Storm felt guilty for a new reason.

"It must be expensive to raise five kids," she said as if she didn't know exactly how expensive it was to raise children. She needed to stop daydreaming about staying in Chance Creek and start figuring out how to fix things back in California.

"It is." Belinda hung several shirts on the sales rack. "Especially when your husband doesn't work steady." She looked down. "Shouldn't have said that," she murmured. "I hate it when women talk down their husbands."

"Darren's not too... happy, is he?" Storm hoped that wasn't a poor choice of words.

"You know what makes men most happy?" Belinda turned to her. "When their work calls to them. When they make enough to provide for their families. Preferably both." She shook her head. "Darren's too worried about money to enjoy his work. Every day I've got some new bill to show him." She flushed, as if she'd revealed too much. "This job will help."

"I promise I won't take chances that are too big," Storm assured her. "Just little ones that might work out really well for both of us." She made herself a new resolution. She would set up the store to be fantastically successful and turn it over to Belinda when it was time for her to go. Knowing she'd helped someone would make the pain of leaving worthwhile.

Belinda grinned at her suddenly. "Everyone's going to come spend their money here anyway just as soon as you open up. You're new. People get bored of the same-old, same-old. You'll do fine."

"THIS CAN'T BE a coincidence," Zane said when he found Mason fixing a flat tire on his truck Friday morning.

"I don't think Darren let the air out of my tire. I hit something when I was driving yesterday—an old tire iron or something. I hoped I got away with it, but I guess I didn't."

"I wouldn't put it past him to have put the tire iron in your way."

Mason stood up, peeling off a work glove. "You think he really has it out for us now?"

"Wouldn't you if you were him?"

"Maybe we should think of a way to head trouble off at the pass."

"Maybe we should find a way to drum him out of town."

Mason grunted. "That's not going to happen. I don't want you escalating this either."

"Yes, sir." Zane's tone was scathing.

Mason just chuckled. "It's about time you understood the hierarchy around here, Private."

"Private, is it?" Zane growled in mock anger. "You just won yourself a round on the obstacle course. You won't be so cocky after I leave you in the dust."

Mason tore off the other glove and followed him toward the woods that housed the course. "You won't be so insubordinate after I leave *you* in the dust."

Austin, standing on the back porch talking to Regan and Ella, spotted them. "Hey!" he hollered. "You racing?"

"You bet!" Mason shouted back.

"I'm in! I'll take on the winner."

"For heaven's sake," Zane heard Ella exclaim to Regan. "Where do they get the energy?"

ONE PROBLEM WITH her working at the store and Zane working on the ranch was that it left them little time to spend together, Storm thought as she was getting dressed that Friday morning. Of course, that was the upside to it as well. Her nighttime interludes with Zane were something special, and they always chatted before they fell asleep, but spending so much time apart meant she had fewer chances to slip up and forget she was supposed to be Kenna.

It was getting harder and harder to keep the pretense up. All of them called her Storm and their talk was about the ranch, the wedding, or Mandy's Emporium. When someone brought up mountain climbing she had to scramble to get back in character again.

Storm glanced at the clock. She was running late if she wanted to reach Mandy's by nine, when she'd told Belinda she'd be there.

"There you are," Regan said, when Storm entered the kitchen for a quick bite a few minutes later. She slid her sleek phone into her purse where it sat on the counter and slung it over her shoulder. "Come on, Storm. We're heading out."

"Great, let me grab a banana. I need a ride to the store."

"Not today. We're going to Billings. Ella, too."

Ella appeared, her purse in her hand. "Everyone ready?"

"Almost. We want to get there right when the stores open," Regan explained to Storm. "We're meeting the guys at the Dancing Boot tonight at nine o'clock. They had to head out to Bozeman to pick up some equipment they can't get in town. They'll eat on the road and meet us at the bar. Mason says we'd better get dolled up, and I'm taking that to mean it's time to buy a new dress. We'll make a day of it."

Storm shook her head. "Sorry, but I can't. I'm supposed to work at the store today."

"You're your own boss and you're not open yet. You can take the day off. By the way, Mia called again yesterday. She said she'd left you a message on your phone but you hadn't called her back." Ella said.

Ella was right, she hadn't called Mia back. If she wasn't going to go into the store, she'd need to call Belinda, too. She knew the other woman would be disappointed if she didn't show up today. "I was really busy yesterday and I still have so much to do. I shouldn't take any time off…"

"Come on, Storm. We've barely gotten to know you yet. Here's our chance." Regan smiled sweetly. "Play hooky from work just this once. We'll help you make up for it tomorrow."

Storm only hesitated a minute. She couldn't resist the invitation without risking them finding out she'd hired Belinda. She wasn't ready for that yet. Besides, she couldn't remember when she'd last spent time shopping and having fun with girlfriends. She'd call Belinda and put her off. She'd get in touch with Mia tomorrow. "Okay."

Belinda was disappointed, but Storm promised to be back to work the next day. That difficult call over, she changed into her best outfit and prepared to enjoy herself. The drive to Billings turned out to be a lot of fun, with Regan and Ella chattering at her. They told her all about their time at the ranch to date, and Storm couldn't believe some of the things that had happened to them.

She wished she would get the chance to know them better. It pained her to know she'd have to leave all of this in late November, but she was determined to enjoy every minute she had here, especially the ones with Zane.

When they got to the first store, Regan immediately took charge. "You've got a pair of boots," she said. "You'll need a hat to go with them, at the very least."

"Oh, I don't think so. I'm not a country girl—I don't want to pretend I am."

Regan rolled her eyes. "I spent the last decade in New York City. Ella spent it in Los Angeles. Look at us now. What makes you any different?"

"I'm just not sure it's me."

Ella chuckled. "It better be you. You're a Hall, now—or you will be soon enough. You'd better start looking like one."

"This is where I got mine," Ella said. "Look—this

one would be perfect on you."

"It would make me look ridiculous."

But she let them bully her into trying one on, secretly liking the attention. She liked the hat too once she had it on. It made her look sassy and sexy and a little bit bad. She just couldn't imagine where she would wear it.

"I need a dress," Regan said. "Something that covers this belly of mine, but still makes me look hot." She sighed. "I'm glad I'm pregnant, but I just don't look the same in a miniskirt, you know?"

"Mason adores you whatever you wear and you know it," Ella said. "I'll be in the same boat in a few months. Don't worry, we'll find you something. I want something new too now that we're here."

Each place they went to, they brought armfuls of clothing into the fitting rooms and traded them back and forth. It reminded Storm of being with her sisters, if her sisters were closer in age. Soon her stiffness and uncertainty had dissolved and she was joking and laughing along with the other two.

"That looks amazing," Ella said when she pulled on a light blue, barely there dress. With a gathered neckline and a baby-doll skirt she looked both young and sensuous.

"What do you guys think about this one?" Regan came out of her fitting room in a short denim skirt with a white ruffled sleeveless shirt that covered the small mound of her belly.

"I love it!" Storm looked her over again. "Sexy, but

not in a sleazy way, you know?"

Ella disappeared inside a room and a moment later came out in a curve-hugging minidress with black and white color blocks that emphasized every one of her attributes.

"You're going to stop traffic in that dress," Regan said. "You need a cherry-red pair of stiletto heels."

"Hmm. Maybe."

Storm suddenly felt underdressed. She looked down at her outfit. Regan caught her. "Uh-uh, don't even think about changing. Trust me—pairing a simple little dress with some cowboy boots will make any country boy swoon."

"If you say so."

By the time they were shopped-out, hunger had kicked in. Regan whipped out her cell phone. "I have an app that finds vegetarian restaurants." They chose a little bistro and were charmed by the cozy ambience. Sharing a platter of hummus and naan to start, they dined on salads and Tex-Mex vegan tacos.

"I've had so much fun today," Storm declared as they climbed back into the truck at the end of their meal.

"I'm glad," Regan said earnestly as she got in the driver's seat. "I was afraid you didn't like us."

"I thought you wouldn't like me," Storm confessed. "And the two of you were like superwomen, getting the chores done before breakfast and all that."

"Well, we wanted to impress you." Ella squeezed in beside her on the front bench seat and Regan started the truck's engine. "Couldn't look like a pair of slackers when the new wife arrives, you know?"

Regan snorted as she backed out of the parking space. "You make it sound like we're sharing one man between us. This isn't Utah."

"We do kind of live on a compound, though. And let's face it—Storm's husband and mine look exactly the same. That's kind of weird, right?"

"They don't look exactly the same." But Storm was giggling, because it *was* weird now that Ella mentioned it.

"What if it was dark?" Regan asked driving toward the highway back to Chance Creek. "Would you be able to tell if they switched places?"

"God, I hope so." Ella stared at Storm in horror. "Austin would never do that."

"Zane wouldn't either." But a thought occurred to Storm. "Do you think they ever did when they were teenagers?"

"Should we ask them?"

All three of them dissolved in laughter.

"Austin would be completely shocked. He's so upright."

"A very good quality in a man," Storm observed.

"I can't take you two anywhere," Regan said, rolling her eyes.

"You can take us to the Dancing Boot," Ella declared. "It's time to get this party started."

"It's a little early. Besides, we need to change."

"I know!" Ella thumped her hand on the dashboard. "The Turners. We'll stop at their ranch, get changed and drag Maya and Stella out with us. It'll be fun. A little mini girls' night out before the guys get there."

"Now that's what I call a plan," Regan said. "Storm, hold onto your brand new hat, baby. It's going to get a little crazy tonight."

CHAPTER TWELVE

"I'M ALWAYS UP for a night on the town, but is there a reason you chose tonight?" Austin asked Zane as they hurried through their evening chores. They'd been gone all day and when they got home there was no sign of the women. They'd decided they'd better get ready to head to the Dancing Boot sooner rather than later.

"I want Storm to like this place as much as I do."

"You got any worries on that score?"

"Not exactly." He searched for the right thing to say. "It's complicated. It's not that I don't want her to climb mountains anymore…"

"It's just that you don't want her to climb mountains anymore," Austin finished for him. "Listen, you can't start a relationship wanting to change the other person."

"I don't want to change her. It'll just be hard to let her go. I mean… what she does is dangerous."

"We better get a move on," Mason hollered, stepping through the barn door.

"What's the rush?"

Mason held out his cell phone. "The girls beat us to the bar. Looks like they're having a little too much fun."

Zane took the phone and grinned at the photo which showed Storm and Ella dancing with Maya and Stella Turner and Camilla Torres, a friend who rented a house on the Turners' ranch. "You're right; we'd better get over there before someone else horns in on our women."

"No one better touch my woman," Austin said. "Let's go."

"THAT WAS PATHETIC," Storm exclaimed, sitting down on the barstool with a thump.

"That was awesome," Ella said, sitting down next to her.

"I can't believe how many people are here tonight." Storm also couldn't believe she'd just tried line-dancing. In public. She'd tripped herself up on her own feet so many times she'd lost count.

"I know, right?" Regan rejoined them after stepping outside to make a call.

There wasn't a band tonight, but the sound system was blasting favorite dance tunes and the floor saw a continual flow of couples and groups having fun. Two booths in the corner were filled with an uproarious crowd of cowboys who seemed to be celebrating something, although Storm couldn't tell what it was. She recognized Darren among them, and avoided making eye contact. She didn't recognize any of the others. A number of single men were drinking at the bar and the door opened to admit another trio of women who looked ready to enjoy themselves.

"I need a drink," Maya Turner cried and the rest of them joined in with a chorus of "Me, too's!" They kept the bartender busy for the next few minutes, Ella and Regan with non-alcoholic choices and the rest of them with beer and mixed drinks. Storm jumped when she felt a man's hand rest proprietarily on her hip.

"Hello there, honey. I don't recognize you."

She looked up to see a man in his late twenties with dark curly hair, a day or two's worth of stubble on his jaw, and sharp gray eyes.

"I'm new to town," she said, trying to extricate herself from his grip.

"Well, I'm not new, but I've just returned from a long absence. I'd forgotten how beautiful the women are around here. The name's Steel. Steel Cooper."

Storm glanced around her for help, but Ella and Regan were deep in conversation several feet away with a couple she didn't recognize, and Maya and Stella had left their drinks on the bar and headed toward the ladies' room.

"It's customary to return the favor when someone introduces himself." The man moved closer.

"I'm Kenna North," she said reluctantly. "Look, I'm waiting for my fiancé." She wasn't sure she liked the looks of this man and she definitely didn't want his hand on her waist.

He captured her hand in his and lifted it. "I don't

see a ring… Kenna."

Kenna's name in his mouth made her even more uncomfortable. "I have to go."

"Now, hold up a minute." He didn't let go of her hand when she tried to walk away. Instead he tugged her toward the dance floor. "I'm only trying to be friendly." She tried to stand her ground, but he was far too strong for her to resist. In another moment she found herself pressed against the cowboy, his arms tightening around her waist.

If Zane was the one holding her, she'd be all too happy to be there, but she didn't like this man or the smell of liquor on his breath. She didn't like the way he kept looking back at the other cowboys in the corner booth and grinning like he'd done something to be proud of. When she glanced over at them she saw Darren laughing.

"I don't want to dance."

"Loosen up a little, baby. I'm just having fun."

"No. I want—"

"Let her go." Suddenly Zane was between them, his broad shoulders forming a barrier between her and the drunken man.

"Says who?"

"Come on, Storm," Regan appeared at her side and led her away from the confrontation, but Storm didn't go too far. It was her fault Zane was facing off with Steel.

"Shouldn't we call the police?"

"Zane will handle it. And if he needs help, Mason

and Austin will stand in." Regan's tone told her she didn't think Zane would need any help.

"Says me." Zane was quiet but firm. Around them the other couples on the floor moved away from the cowboys. "That's my woman, and she doesn't want to dance with you."

"Hell, she wants to do more than dance. Did you see the way she was looking at my—"

Zane's fist connected with Steel's cheek with a crack that silenced the bar. Steel lobbed back a punch that glanced off Zane's shoulder.

"Ohmygod!" Storm searched the rest of the crowd. Wasn't anyone going to stop them?

Zane struck back with another crushing blow that sent Steel sprawling to the ground. The corner booth erupted with angry cowboys and in a second the dance floor was overrun with men making a beeline toward Zane. Mason and Austin jumped into the fray to meet them, followed closely by more cowboys she didn't recognize.

"It's the Turners! Maya and Stella's brothers and cousins!" Regan pointed at the melee, pulling Storm back even further.

Storm narrowed her eyes when she saw Darren moving against the tide. What was he doing? For a moment she thought he meant to take advantage of the crowd to score an unfair hit or two on one of the Halls, but she quickly realized he meant to slip away out of the club altogether.

Good riddance.

Storm lost sight of him, and understood Regan meant the Turners were the extra cowboys who were fighting on Zane's side. Twisting around, she saw the bartender punching numbers into his cellphone and she hoped he was calling the police, even as she feared if he was, Zane and his brothers would end up in trouble.

She shrieked when someone threw a chair and it splintered against the wall.

"Get back," Ella cried, grabbing both of them and pushing them along the bar into the rear part of the club. "This is out of control."

"Do they do this a lot?" Storm shouted over the din.

"I've never seen them do it before," Regan said. "Mason's broken up a couple of fights, but he's never been in one."

Storm didn't like this one bit. "What if they're hurt?"

Ella just shook her head and the three of them clung together while all around them chaos reigned. When several men in uniform burst in a few moments later, Storm gasped with relief. The shouting continued between the two parties of men, but the officers separated them and put a stop to the fighting.

"Well, this is going to take forever to sort out," Ella said with the air of someone who'd seen a barroom brawl before. "We might as well find a table. I'll grab you another drink, Storm."

Her prediction turned out to be right. They sat for another hour before the Sheriff's deputies sorted out the mess, collared a few of the men to take to the station and let the rest go. Zane shuffled over, battered but triumphant. "Steel will think twice before he tries that again."

Storm just shook her head. His lip was split, his cheek bruised, and his knuckles were swelling. "I can't believe you fought them."

"What did you want me to do, stand back and watch him paw you?" He held up a hand and a passing waitress came by. "Get me a beer, would you?"

"Sure thing. Nice work, Zane."

"Thanks."

Storm rolled her eyes. "Nice work?"

"Honey, this is the country. It's not all rules and etiquette here. Sometimes we just throw down and sort things out the old-fashioned way."

"Been a long time since I was in a good fight," Mason said. He looked downright cheerful, even though he was sporting a black eye.

"Wedding photos," Regan suddenly cried. "Oh, my goodness—look at the lot of you. You'll look a mess in those photos and you're paying a pretty penny for them, Zane."

Zane laughed. "That's weeks away. We'll be fine by then, and if not, we'll just look manly in them."

"Did someone say manly?" A cowboy Storm didn't know pulled up a seat and joined them, trailed by several other men, and Maya and Stella.

"Storm, these are the Turner boys," Zane said. "Noah and Liam are Maya and Stella's brothers. Eli,

Brody and Alex are cousins who've come to help run their ranch."

"Hi." Storm did her best to memorize their faces and names, but she'd had several drinks tonight and a moment later she couldn't remember which of the tall, blue-eyed, dark haired men was Liam and which was Noah. Eli's sandy-brown hair and mischievous smirk made more of an impression, but as for Brody and Alex—she'd already forgotten who was whom. Her head was spinning and she was feeling a bit unsteady. She noticed the music had come back on and couples were taking to the dance floor again. Eli glanced that way, then back at Storm. His grin broadened and he drawled, "Want to dance, little lady?"

Zane slugged him good-naturedly in the shoulder. "Back off, Turner. I think I've made it clear tonight she's all mine." He held out his hand to Storm. She took it and let him lead her to the floor. When he put his arms around her, she sagged against him.

"I think I've had a little too much to drink," she confessed, pressing her cheek against his chest. She liked it here. Liked him holding her tight.

He drew her closer. "You're perfect."

Storm smiled against the fabric of his cotton shirt. "I can barely stand up."

"You don't have to do a thing. Just let me do all the work."

He did, too, weaving them around the floor slowly, swaying in time to the beat, rocking her back and forth until Storm grew sleepy. Sometime later he murmured,

"I think it's time to get you home."

"Mmm. Sounds good."

He scooped her right up in his arms. Storm cuddled against him happily as he made his way back toward the rest of their party. "We're out of here. See you all back at the ranch."

"Night! See you later!" A chorus of good-byes washed over her, and then Zane turned toward the front door. Someone held it open for them and when they got outside, Zane helped her to a truck she recognized as Mason's. He deposited her in her seat, got in on his own side and then pulled her close against him. She liked riding like this through the country night, her head resting on Zane's shoulder. He felt strong and safe next to her. Trustworthy. The thought of ever leaving Chance Creek felt like it would break her heart.

"Come on, honey. Let's get inside," Zane said when they arrived. He helped her into the Hall and up the stairs.

As soon as they were in their bedroom, she turned to face him, teetering in her boots as the room spun. "Aren't you going to kiss me?"

He chuckled and moved in closer. "Of course I am." He bent down and captured her mouth with his and kissed her until her knees buckled. When he finally released her, she had to cling to his shirt to stay upright.

"Help me out of this?" She turned around and lifted her hair. "I've got something new on underneath," she crooned. "I put it on just for you."

"Then let's see it." The hunger in his voice made her smile. Zane was always hungry for her.

He smoothed a tendril of her hair aside and slowly unzipped her dress, peeling it off of her and letting it fall to the ground. Beneath it she wore a bra and panty set the other women had convinced her to buy. She was glad now that she had. She felt sexy. Wicked, even. Zane would definitely want to touch her.

"What do you think?" She stretched luxuriously and something in his eyes darkened. He kissed her again, tangling a hand in her hair and circling her waist with his other hand.

"You're beautiful. As always."

"I'm still wearing too many clothes."

"You need help with those, too?"

She nodded. He carefully undid the clasp of her bra and pushed the straps off her shoulders. Storm closed her eyes, let the bra fall away, and leaned into his touch, desperate to feel his hands on her skin.

When he whispered, "Time for bed," a few moments later, Storm moaned in anticipation. Yes, that was exactly what she wanted—to be in bed with Zane. She watched him pull the covers off and shimmied out of her panties. When he held up the covers she climbed in, desperate to pull him close.

He removed his close and sat on the edge of the bed, the mattress sinking beneath his weight. "Why hasn't some man snatched you up before now?"

"I've been too busy."

"Lucky for me." He cupped both her breasts, smoothing his palms over her nipples. Storm leaned back against the pillows as he bent to take one into his mouth. He toyed with her until she arched her back. When he moved to her other breast, Storm moaned. She couldn't get enough of this. She thought she could make love to Zane for all eternity and still want him again.

Lying back against the pillows, her head spinning, she made a resolution. She wouldn't give Zane back to Kenna. She wouldn't leave Chance Creek. She wanted this life; Kenna didn't. Kenna could find her own husband.

Zane pressed himself against her so she could feel how much he wanted her. She angled herself to meet him, sliding her hands over his hips and digging her fingers into his skin. When he kissed his way lower— much lower—she surrendered to his touch with a little cry. Burying her hands in his thick, short hair she allowed him access to the innermost parts of her. She was never shy with Zane. She shifted underneath him, moaning as he teased her.

When it was clear she was close to losing control, Zane moved to settle himself between her legs, but when he reached for a condom, Storm caught his wrist. "No."

"Storm—"

"No. I want this to be real. I want to be your wife. I want your baby."

"Honey, you're drunk. You have plans for your

life—big ones."

"I'm changing them right now, with you. I want this more."

He hesitated. "You know that's what I want, too, but I'm not going to let you—"

"Who said I was giving you a choice?" Was he going to deny her what she really wanted? Why did the world always conspire to stand against her? When had she ever done exactly as she pleased?

"Storm?" Zane was concerned.

"I want you. Please. Don't make me leave you."

"No one's ever going to make you leave if you don't want to," he assured her, gathering her in close.

"Yes, they will. You don't understand."

Storm didn't wait for Zane to make up his mind. She shifted beneath him until he was close to entering her. She gripped his hips and tugged at him, trying to pull him inside her.

"Storm." He captured her wrists, pinning them against the mattress. He was far too strong for her to fight. "You have to tell me this is what you really want."

"It's what I want," she said.

"To be with me forever?"

"Yes."

"To have my children?"

"Yes."

"To be my wife?"

She nodded, wanting him with every fiber of her being—wanting everything he was offering, too. She wanted to be tied so tightly to him that nothing could tear them apart. And if nothing else, she wanted to feel him inside her with nothing between them. She deserved that much, at least.

Zane hesitated so long she thought she'd lost him and she closed her eyes, a tear escaping from under her lids, so when he pressed inside her, she gasped and arched her back. Zane pulled her close with a groan. "I want you too. I want you so much." He kissed her hungrily, stroking into her again. He'd always turned her on, but with nothing between them, the sensation was wholly new. Just knowing that he could make her pregnant tonight made her throb with need. His ragged breathing was loud in her ears and she gripped the comforter as he plunged deep inside her. He felt so right between her legs. As she whispered encouragement, he began to move.

He started slowly, but Storm wasn't having any of that. She wrapped her legs around his waist and begged him for more. He thrust faster, deeper, increasing his pace until she could barely hold on.

When she came, Storm cried out and buried her face in his neck, her breath rasping in and out with her smothered words. Heat and sensation exploded inside her and Zane bucked against her, his own muffled grunts coming fast and hard. Wave after wave of pleasure washed over her until she didn't know where she began and Zane ended. When he was done, Zane collapsed on top of her and they both fought to regain their breath.

He kissed her again, under her ear, over her forehead and on her lips.

She clung to him, never wanting to let him go.

As his breathing slowed, he pulled out and rolled over until they both lay on their sides. As he wrapped his arms around her, she could hear his heartbeat loud in his chest. She knew he'd been as swept away as she was.

He murmured something into her hair as they lay there entwined, but Storm couldn't make out his words. "What?" she breathed.

"I love you."

Her eyes pricked with tears as she pressed herself closer. "I love you, too."

CHAPTER THIRTEEN

"**D**ID YOU HAVE fun last night?" Austin said when Zane met him in the barn the following morning.

Fun didn't even come close to describing it. He bit back a telltale smile at the memory, then sobered again. "Yeah. Could do without the bumps and bruises, but it was worth it." Last night had been the best of his life so far, but this morning Zane's guilt was gnawing at him. He'd taken advantage of Storm in all kinds of ways—especially by letting her convince him to have unprotected sex. He should have waited until she was sober to make such a momentous move. She had a career to consider—one she'd previously made clear was her top priority. She'd been swept away by the moment. After a fun afternoon with Regan and Ella, she'd been well on her way to hammered before he even made it to the bar. Then he'd defended her honor when Steel harassed her. He must have looked like a hero to her at one in the morning, but how would he look today?

Would she still want him? Or would she hate his

guts?

"Something wrong?" Austin asked.

"No. Just something I need to sort out with Storm."

"Sort out. That doesn't sound good."

"It's fine. Everything's fine."

Austin didn't look like he believed him. Zane wished he could convince himself.

WHEN STORM WOKE, her tongue thick in a mouth so dry it propelled her out of her bed and into the bathroom for a drink of water, neither her pounding head nor the queasy feeling in her belly could dampen her happiness.

She'd slept with Zane without a condom. She rested a hand on her belly and wondered if she was pregnant even now, growing a new child within her that would link her to Zane forever.

That was probably wishful thinking, she decided as she squinted at her reflection in the mirror, grateful Zane couldn't see her now. There were bags under her eyes and her hair looked like she'd combed it with an egg-beater, but a smile lifted a corner of her mouth as she searched for pain reliever in the cabinet. She didn't look forward to the conversation she'd have to have with Kenna, but she wouldn't let that get her down. Making love to Zane had become her favorite thing to do. The sweet soreness between her legs reminded her of the way she'd thrown caution to the wind and met his passion headlong with her own. She hadn't held

158 | CORA SETON

back, hadn't pretended not to care for him. In fact, she'd declared her love to him.

She wanted to do it again.

When her phone trilled, she picked it up, saw her mother's name and almost didn't answer it, but guilt followed quickly, and she tapped to accept the call.

"Hi, Mom."

"They took my car."

"What? Who did?"

"The bank. They just came and repossessed my car. I'm at work! Now what am I supposed to do?"

Her shrill voice cutting through the line made Storm wince. "Take a taxi home and get mine. It's paid off and it's not like I'm using it."

"That's not the point! The point is I need more money. You should be here—"

Guilt squeezed Storm's gut again. She'd been so caught up in her own happiness with Zane, she'd almost forgotten how Cheyenne must be struggling back in California. Her problems would get worse when Storm informed Kenna that their deal was off. Kenna wouldn't pay her bonus—the bonus Cheyenne was depending on to square her debts.

Which led her to another problem. She'd married Zane as Kenna. Did that mean he needed to divorce Kenna in order to be able to marry her for real? Storm clutched the phone as she thought that through. And how would Zane react when he found out that she'd tricked him? Would he understand, or would he be furious?

Would he stop loving her?

She placed a hand over her belly again, willing there to be a baby growing inside her to link them together no matter what happened. But no, that wasn't fair to Zane, or the baby—

"It's so hard!" Cheyenne kept on talking. "You don't know what it's like—"

Something snapped in Storm. She *did* know what it was like. She'd worked by her mother's side for eight years, stepping straight into her father's shoes when she was barely fifteen years old. What right had Cheyenne to commandeer her childhood like that? She should have been hanging out with her friends, meeting boys—surfing. Instead she'd started what already felt like a lifetime of work.

"Mom, stop it."

Cheyenne broke off. "What did you say to me?"

"I said it's time to stop complaining about money. I'm sorry that you're in this predicament, but you don't need to be. Sell the house. You'll be set for years—until after the girls grow up. Meanwhile figure out what you want to do with your life and train to do it."

"Sell the house? What about your bonus?"

"Are you listening to yourself? You're right; it's *my* bonus. I'm twenty-three years old. I'm supposed to be making my own family, not supporting yours."

"You're not even dating anyone!"

"News flash, Mom. I'm married, remember? To Zane Hall, Kenna's cowboy. And there isn't going to be any bonus because I plan to stay married to him."

"I can't believe... I don't..."

"Believe it. I'm not your husband, Mom. I'm your daughter."

"The most ungrateful daughter who ever lived!"

"Mom." Storm struggled for the courage to complete the conversation. "If you really needed me, I'd always be there for you. You don't need me, though. What you need is to let go of the past and move on. We can't keep the house."

With a cry, Cheyenne hung up, leaving Storm to brace herself against the wave of shame that crashed over her a moment later. How could she say those things to her mother?

Even if they were true?

"ARE YOU GOING into town today?" Zane asked later when they met on the stairs. She'd spent the intervening time trying to plan her next move. Should she call Kenna? Or talk to Zane? Or see a lawyer? She didn't know where to start.

"I plan to if I can get a ride."

"Come find me if no one else is going in and I'll see that you get there." He hesitated. "Are we... okay after last night?"

"I want to be." Sadness pierced her at how complicated it had all become.

"I'd like to kiss you but I'm worried you think I took advantage of you."

He looked so appealing standing one riser down so that they were practically face to face. Worry shadowed his handsome features and she longed to kiss it away. She chuckled. "I think I might be the one who took advantage."

He hooked his thumbs in the waistband of her jeans and pulled her close. He kissed her softly yet thoroughly until Storm's body woke up and wanted more. "I've got to get back to work, but I meant what I said last night. I do love you."

"I love you, too."

"Find me if you need a ride."

"I will."

She walked the rest of the way downstairs slowly, her whole body tingling, and found Ella and Regan in the kitchen, as they usually were at this time of day. They seemed to be moving as slowly as she was and they joined her at the table to eat.

"Was that a normal Friday night around here?" Storm asked them as she got her breakfast.

"All except the bar fight; that was a new one," Ella said.

"I can do without that happening again," Regan put in.

"You and Zane looked like you were having fun." Ella took a bite of her cereal.

Storm shrugged, hoping they wouldn't press her further on that topic. Her love for Zane was far too new to share with anyone. "I think I'll go into town today to work on the store a little."

"If you can wait a half-hour, I'll drive you." Regan smiled. "I have a hair appointment this morning."

"I'll be in town later this afternoon if you need a ride home," Ella said.

"Thanks." Storm appreciated their offers but she was beginning to feel like a teenager whose social life had outstripped her mobility. Zane had said he meant to purchase a truck now that he was home for good, but that still left her without a set of wheels to call her own. If she was going to stay here much longer, she needed to get a car. She thought of the one she'd left in California. She guessed that was Cheyenne's now.

A knock on the front door interrupted their conversation. Ella went to open it and Storm and Regan followed her.

"Hi Heather. Hi Richard," Ella said. "The men are already at work, if you want to find them."

The tall boy was off like a shot. His mother—as Storm presumed the curvy blonde to be—remained on the stoop. She was dressed in jeans that hugged every contour and a pretty sweater that made the most of her figure. "Thanks. He couldn't wait to get over here today. I had to force him to wait for a decent hour."

"He can come any time he likes. Besides, the men are up before daylight—you know that."

"I figure it's best to give them a few hours to shake off their Friday night before I inflict Richard on them on a Saturday morning," Heather said. She looked at Storm curiously. "I haven't seen you before. Are you Zane's fiancée?"

Storm nodded.

"I'm Heather. Richard is Colt's son."

"Oh." Storm wasn't sure of the proper etiquette in this situation. "It's nice that Richard likes to spend time with his uncles."

Some kind of significant look passed between the other women, but Storm didn't know what it meant. "Yes, it is," Heather said. "Well, I'm off to the hardware store."

"Are you going into town?" Storm jumped at the chance not to be a burden to Regan and Ella. "I could use a ride if you are."

"Sure." Heather recovered from her surprise at the request quickly. "I wouldn't mind at all."

"Thanks—I'll just grab my purse."

She said good-bye to the other women and assured them she'd make her own way home, then climbed thankfully into Heather's truck. She rested her head against the back of the seat, still woozy from the previous night. "I really need a car."

"I'll bet. It's not convenient to live in the country without your own vehicle."

Now that they were alone, Storm was fully aware of the awkwardness of the situation. "I'm sorry I ambushed you—asking for a ride like that."

"No problem. You aren't having trouble with Miss Perfect One and Two back there, are you?"

"No! Not at all. It's just…" Storm examined her emotions. "I feel so useless around them. They have this ranch wife business all sewn up. Meanwhile, I'm flailing around like a beached dolphin. I don't even know what I'm doing here."

"Marrying Zane, presumably." Heather shot her another curious look.

"Right. Of course."

"Is everything all right between you?"

"It's getting there." She laughed uncomfortably. "You'd think we'd already be there with our wedding coming up, wouldn't you?" She closed her eyes, realizing she still hadn't called Mia Matheson. The wedding planner must be frantic. Or maybe she'd stopped making any plans.

Heather sighed. "Love can be rough. From what I've heard, though, Zane really adores you."

"Really?" What had she heard? And from whom?

"This is a small town. People talk—a lot. There aren't many secrets around here."

Storm twisted her hands in her lap. She wondered what people were saying about her.

"Someone told me Steel Cooper tried to hit on you last night and Zane came in swinging."

"And that's the local definition of true love?"

"No. The local wisdom is based on the way Zane danced with you afterward. Like he couldn't hold you close enough, was how Renee Peterson put it. Look, I'm not going to tell you how to run your life—I just met you. What I do know is that the Hall men are pretty special. When one of them falls in love with you, you want to hold onto that."

It was Storm's turn to look curiously at Heather. "You said Colt was Richard's father, but you didn't say he was your husband."

"He's not." Heather's expression turned grim. "We were together when we were teenagers. It was just... stupid. It should never have happened. I used to date Austin—for a long time."

"Oh." That explained the atmosphere back at the ranch. "So you weren't in love with Colt?"

Heather's glance held a world of pain. "I was. I loved him so much. I just couldn't have him."

"Oh, Heather." Suddenly her own problems seemed trivial in comparison. At least she had a choice if she wanted to be with Zane or not. Heather would probably give anything to be in her position. She remembered Heloise's requirements for the brothers. "He's going to get married before the deadline..."

"Not to me."

Storm's heart ached for the other woman. "But you're the mother of his child, and you love him. Does he know that?"

Heather shook her head. "He can't bear to think about me. I broke up with Austin before I was with Colt, but we both still felt like we were doing something wrong. And then their father died all of a sudden. It was so awful. Colt felt like it was his fault—like if he hadn't been with me, it wouldn't have happened. It makes no sense but it's all tangled up together, our sneaking around and his father's death. When they left Chance Creek and I found out I was pregnant, I never told anyone who the father was. Colt doesn't even know."

"Why haven't you told him?"

"His unit is on some kind of a mission and he can't communicate with anyone. We don't know when he'll be in touch again. When he is back online, I'm going to try something a little devious."

They had reached the town, and Storm broke in to tell her she was going to Mandy's. "What are you going to try?"

"You know about the wife wanted ad, of course— the one Mason put up for all of them?"

"Yes." Zane had told her about that, although the one Kenna had answered was apparently a different one he'd written himself.

"I'm going to answer his with a fake name. I'm going to try to make him fall in love with me again."

Misgivings filled Storm. "Is that a good idea?"

"I don't know." Heather pulled into a parking space in front of the store. "It's the only idea I've got."

"You could tell him the truth."

"I don't think so. Not if I want to stand a chance."

"Well, good luck then. I really hope it goes the way you want it to."

"I hope so, too." She peered out the truck's windshield at the store. "This is yours now?"

"For the time being, at least. I hope to have it up and running soon."

"Let me know if you need any help."

"I will." Storm climbed out and shut the door behind her, still thinking about Heather's situation. As she fumbled with her purse, looking for her key, Belinda came around the corner. "Hi, Belinda," Storm called, finally locating her key ring. She pulled it out and unlocked the door. "Are you coming in?"

Belinda came closer. "I wasn't sure if you'd want me to."

"Why not?"

"Because of the way Darren behaved last night. I wasn't there," she went on, "but I heard all about it. How he got Steel to hit on you."

"He got Steel to do that?" Storm was bewildered by all the undercurrents in the relationships around her. She thought back to the night before. Realized she couldn't remember exactly how the fight had started. "I just thought Steel was drunk."

"I'm sure he was. Those Coopers are a handful at the best of times. I wish they'd never moved back to town."

"Well, I don't hold you accountable for anything Steel or Darren did." She led the way inside. "What does Darren think about you working here?" The mustiness of the store washed over her as always and she wrinkled her nose. "Let's keep the door open for now and see if there are any windows we can open too. It'll be cool, but it's a nice day and at least it will smell better."

"Should we go back to sorting clothes?"

Storm nodded.

"Darren doesn't know I'm working here." Belinda made a face. "You must think my husband is awful. Even his own wife lies to him."

"I don't know Darren. I'm sure you have a good

reason for not telling him." Storm hoped that was diplomatic enough. From everything she'd heard and seen she couldn't imagine why Belinda put up with the man.

"Darren was always wild. I was too," Belinda confessed. "We both got pegged as troublemakers when we were young and now we can't seem to get past it. I love our kids, I really do, but with five of them we're always scraping by. For years I couldn't work outside the house because we couldn't afford daycare. Now that they're in school, I have no skills."

"It'll get better, I'm sure." The words sounded trite to her own ears. Her phone chimed, but when she pulled it out, she saw it was Mia Matheson and she let it go to voice mail.

"I don't know. Darren's in construction and that's not such a great line of work these days. And with his reputation it's hard to get jobs. He'll show up somewhere and the foreman will say, 'I remember that time you ran your truck right into a ditch.'" She held up her hands. "That happened when Darren was sixteen. He's never been in another accident."

"That's rough." Storm had lived all her life in Santa Cruz, a medium-sized town on its own, but it was surrounded with other towns and larger cities, so there was always a stream of new people moving through. Funny how she'd had the same experience, though, getting stuck living at home to keep her mother happy, and having her self-esteem undercut daily by the way Kenna treated her. It occurred to her now that she could have chosen to surround herself with other people—new people who might have supported her own goals. People who didn't know about her past and so held no expectations for her future.

Like the people here.

She turned that thought over in her mind. It was true; they'd heard she was a mountain climber, but they hadn't formed a strong opinion of who she was or what she was capable of. She could be anything she wanted to be. She looked around the store. She could transform this place into anything she wanted it to be, too. She touched a rack of clothing, letting the cool metal rod assure her this was all real.

"You can change. So can Darren," she said aloud. "It's harder when you're surrounded by people who've always known you, but you can do it."

"You think so?" Belinda sounded interested.

"I'm sure of it."

CHAPTER FOURTEEN

W HEN HIS PHONE chimed, Zane leaned his
pitchfork against Jasper's stall wall and fished it
out of his pocket. Heloise. Just what he needed.

He knew his aunt wasn't to be ignored, though, so
he accepted the call and held the phone to his ear.
"How's my favorite aunt?"

"Cut the baloney," she snapped. "You've got a
problem."

"What problem?"

Mason, passing through, stopped to listen. "What's
wrong?"

Zane waved him off, then rolled his eyes when
Austin appeared, too. The only thing worse than
dealing with an angry Heloise was dealing with her with
an audience.

"Just how well do you know that fiancée of yours?"

Zane's stomach sunk. Could Heloise have discovered their trick? Which wasn't a trick anymore as far as
he was concerned. "Well enough. Why?"

"I doubt you know her as well as you think you do.
Either that or you're pulling a fast one on me. Which is

it?"

"Why don't you tell me what it is you think *you* know, Heloise. I don't have time for games. I've got shit to scoop."

"Don't get crude with me, young man."

"Spill it, Heloise."

"Fine. I'll spill it. Kenna North is currently in Nepal climbing some mountain called Lhotse." She spelled it out. "So who is that woman living with you?"

"I have no idea what you're talking about. Where are you getting this stuff?"

She huffed. "There's this new-fangled thing called the Internet. Maybe you should check it out. I don't appreciate being made a fool of. If you've tried to pull a fast one, this deal is off. Darren was telling me just the other day he would love to inherit Crescent Hall." She cut the call, leaving Zane to stare at his phone in bewilderment.

"What was that all about?" Mason said.

"She said... it makes no sense."

"What did she say?"

"Kenna—Storm—is in Nepal on a climbing expedition. She saw it on the Internet."

Both his brothers stared at him.

"If Kenna's in Nepal, then who are you engaged to?" Austin demanded.

"I don't know. Kenna! Storm. Whoever she is. Heloise must have gotten it wrong." But worry still twisted his gut. Could Storm be an imposter? Why would she pose as someone else? He remembered the photograph—the one that barely looked like her and a chill raced down his spine. Had she been lying to him this whole time?

"Her arms," Mason broke in suddenly. "It's always bothered me. It's fall, so she usually wears long sleeves, but when she rolls them up she's not muscular enough."

"She's way too small," Austin agreed. "She couldn't pull her weight on an expedition. Mason's right. If she was a climber, she'd be muscle all over."

Zane was staggered by the way they were echoing the doubts that plagued his own mind. He knew Storm's body better than anyone. Why hadn't he thought about her lack of muscle-tone? Was it because he wanted so badly to believe her story? "Then who is she?"

"You met her online, right?" Mason said.

He nodded.

"She could be anyone. It's not like you checked her ID."

Hope pierced through Zane. "Yes, I did." At his brothers' startled looks he went on. "Not me, exactly. But the man who married us did." When Austin's eyebrows shot up, he took a deep breath and spilled it all. "We were wed at the Chance Creek county courthouse right before I brought her to meet you."

"Why?" Mason asked.

"Because..." He trailed off. The earth tilted a fraction beneath his feet as he remembered what Storm had said. She wasn't sure she could carry off the deception that they were marrying for real.

"Hey," Austin said. "You all right?"

"Yeah." But he wasn't sure that was true. He felt like his favorite horse had just kicked him in the ribs. Storm had wanted to be sure she could leave Chance Creek at any time. Was that because she was afraid of being found out?

His brothers were still watching him and he knew he had to come clean. What happened now affected all of them. "I couldn't find a wife," he began and told them everything.

STORM NOTICED THAT today Belinda had made more of an effort with her appearance. She still wore jeans and boots, but her top was a trendy blouse and her hair was done up with a scarf tied around it to hide most of her roots. Her makeup was as impeccable as ever and she worked so efficiently Storm thought she had the makings of a terrific employee—and maybe owner someday, if things fell apart and Storm left on schedule after Thanksgiving.

She didn't like thinking about that, so she got to work taking down the musty old curtains that framed the wide front window. She ran down to the grocery store, stocked up on cleaning supplies and scrubbed all the glass until it shone. Belinda kept working on sorting the clothes. She was doing a good job of it.

"That's much better," Belinda said an hour later, surveying Storm's handiwork. "It was like being in a tomb before."

"The curtains held in the smell, too. I bet this carpet isn't much better." The color—a dingy brown—was certainly horrendous. She moved to a corner and pried up a bit. "Oh my gosh—there's hardwood underneath it."

"I'm not surprised." Belinda didn't even come to see. "All the older shops in this part of town had wooden floors back in the day."

Storm had a flash of how the store could look with gleaming floors, a fresh coat of paint on the walls and light streaming in all over. She could do this—she could provide Chance Creek with a terrific women's clothing store.

She caught sight of Belinda watching her. "What?"

"You just lit up like a Christmas tree."

Storm grinned. "That's because this place is going to be fantastic."

Belinda rolled her eyes. "I could have told you that."

Storm pulled the carpet back some more. It came away from the floor with a satisfying rip.

"Are you going to take that up right now?"

"I want to." She looked around the room and took in all the racks of clothing sitting on top of the carpet. "I guess I can't though. Not until our sale."

"When are we going to start the sale?"

"As soon as possible," Storm decided. "Maybe next week."

Belinda took a deep breath. "Okay." She didn't sound pleased, though. Storm realized Darren was the problem. As soon as they opened, people would see her and gossip would get back to him.

"Do you want me to put it off a few days?"

"No." Belinda waved that off. "I have to tell him sometime, I guess." She obviously wasn't looking forward to it. Storm wondered if she'd still have a helper after Belinda did. Would Darren prevent his wife from working here?

They got back to work and by noontime they'd made a lot of progress. Belinda would need to leave in a minute, but she had just taken an armful of clothes they meant to keep into the back room when the front door swung open and Zane walked in, looking like thunder.

Storm stopped, arms deep in a pile of unfashionable jeans she was moving to a nearby rack. "Hey. What are you doing here?"

"We need to talk." He scanned the store. "What are you doing with all of this stuff?"

"I'm going to have a tag sale next week," she said, frowning at his tone. "I want to clear everything out and start over with up-to-date merchandise."

He spotted the corner where she'd torn away the carpet. Crossed to it. "What happened here?"

"That's hardwood underneath. I'm planning to rip up the carpet and refinish it."

"Oh, yeah?" He glanced around again. "What else are you going to do?"

Why did he sound so angry? A tendril of fear wound its way through her. "I'll paint the walls, of course," she said slowly. "Something lighter. Brighten up the place. These sales racks need to be moved, too."

"Sounds like you have a lot of plans for the place," he said, coming toward her. Storm watched him warily. Zane had never acted like this before with her and she didn't like it. "So tell me, did you ever plan—"

"Oh, I'm sorry. I'm just back for another load," Belinda said, coming out of the store room.

Zane whirled around. "Belinda?" He turned back to Storm, incredulous. "What the hell is she doing here? Is she part of your trick? Did she put you up to it?" When Storm didn't answer, he swung around again. "God damn it, Belinda—you and Darren take the cake. Get out of here. Go!" He pointed toward the door.

Belinda's face crumpled and she ran for it, grabbing her purse as she fled. Storm scrambled to follow her. "Wait! Belinda! Zane, what the hell?"

"What do you mean, what the hell? You're all in this together, aren't you! All of you trying to destroy me!"

"Because I invited Belinda here to help?" He wasn't making sense.

"You invited her? Don't you mean she invited you? You pretend to love me while all the while working for the man who wants to steal my ranch? What the fuck?" He kicked a rack aside.

Storm scrambled backwards. "I'm not working for Darren. I'm prepping Belinda to help me run the store. When I leave she's going to take it over."

Zane pulled back, his face hardening into a mask of

anger. "When you *leave?*"

"*If* I leave. I mean… you know what I mean!"

"Yeah, I know what you mean. You've been bull-shitting me this whole time. You've been setting me up. You and Darren and Belinda. You want my home. You want my ranch. Well, guess what? You're not going to get it."

"Zane!"

"You know what? I don't want to hear it! Not one word." Zane put up a hand to stop her. "Here's the way things are going to go from now on. You're working for me now and you're going to act your socks off when you're at the ranch or we're around other people. Otherwise, you keep the hell away from me. Don't think I'll touch you again, either. I can't believe—" He ran a hand through his hair and turned away, his disgust plain to see. He stalked toward the front door. "By the way, this store isn't yours to give to anyone—certainly not to the family who made my family's life a living hell. When the time's up and you're gone, you're just gone."

CHAPTER FIFTEEN

ZANE SWUNG THE axe with all his might, grunting when the blade bit into wood. The pile of split logs by his feet was growing by the minute, but his anger wasn't diminishing at all as the crisp smell of wood chips blended with the other scents of a cool fall day.

Storm had lied to him from the start—about everything. Who she was, why she was there, who she worked for—

That she wanted a baby.

He swung the axe again.

He'd fucked her without a condom. No—even now he couldn't use that word to characterize what he'd done. He wasn't the villain here. He hadn't fucked her; he'd made love to her. Because he'd thought he *had* loved her.

What he loved was a lie.

He wasn't sure which infuriated him more, that she'd played him so hard he'd lost his head over her, or that Darren had been clever enough to pull this off. Hell, he'd been surprised that the man would have the gumption to tamper with his pasture fence. This—this was something else.

Zane stopped.

This was beyond Darren.

He leaned on the axe, feeling suddenly ill at ease. That was the truth of it; his cousin wasn't dumb, but he wasn't worldly, either. He had never left Chance Creek, and he still worked a job that he'd picked up as a teenager. Formulating this plan had taken a level of sophistication he couldn't credit to the man. Storm had identification that hadn't tripped up the Judge one bit, and he figured Masters was someone who'd seen his share of ID's.

So who was Storm really? Why was she here?

When I'm gone. She'd tossed off the phrase so casually, as if nothing different had ever been on the table. As if they weren't married already. As if they hadn't pledged their love to each other just last night.

As if he didn't mean a thing to her.

"What are you going to do now?"

Zane swung around when Austin approached.

"I don't know. I went to the store to confront Storm and Belinda was there. Storm hired her, for crying out loud, so I jumped to the only conclusion I could—that Darren set this all up."

Austin cocked his head. "Darren? What, you think he saw your wife-wanted ad and hired Storm to answer it? That seems a bit out of his league, don't you think?"

"Yeah. I do now that I've had time to think about it."

"This is a goddamn mess."

"You don't have to tell me that."

"You've got to fix it."

"Wish I knew how."

"Figure it out."

Austin was angry and he couldn't blame him. They both turned to face the Hall. If he lost them the ranch again through his own stupidity…

"I'll get it done—somehow." He'd set Storm straight on what he expected from her. He'd get through the next few months somehow. He'd convince Heloise to sign the papers over for the goddamn ranch. Then—

Then he'd let Storm go and hope he never saw her again.

STORM STAYED AT the store as long as possible, but when the shadows grew thick outside her door and traffic thinned out, she knew she had to face the music. She'd long since cried herself dry. Her throat ached, her eyes stung, but more was yet to come. She didn't know what she'd find back at the ranch. Her only consolation was that she doubted she could feel worse than she did now.

She gathered her things, called a taxi and waited by the front window. All her joy in owning a store was gone. Coming to Chance Creek had been a big mistake.

The cabbie tried to chat as he drove down the country highway south of town, but Storm couldn't focus. She hesitated at the base of the Hall's steps when they arrived, wishing she didn't have to go inside. If only she had told Zane right from the start about her plan to hire Belinda. She should have trusted him to be able to talk it through, although judging from his reaction today, could he really blame her that she hadn't?

Yes, she decided in the end. He could. She kept trying to circumvent her problems rather than dealing with them head on. Why was that?

She traced her hand along the worn wooden railing of the front stairs. It didn't take a genius to figure that out, she decided. Cheyenne did the same thing. They were two of a kind.

She resolved to find Zane, explain the sequence of events that had led to her hiring Belinda on the sly and promise him it wouldn't happen again. Before she could climb the steps, however, headlights flashed across the Hall and another taxi drove in behind her. She waited until it pulled to a stop in front of the house. The rear door flung open and a small shape exited it. "Storm!"

"Zoe?" Storm couldn't believe her eyes. "Daisy? Violet? What are you doing here?"

Cheyenne was the last to exit the cab. "Since you've decreed I have to give up my home, we've come to stay with you," she announced.

ZANE BREATHED A sigh of relief when the front door opened and Storm walked in. He'd half convinced himself she'd leave Chance Creek directly and he'd never see her again. If that was the case, he should have been happy, but he knew he'd be anything but. As angry as he was, he wanted answers. The only person who could give them to him was Storm.

He rose to his feet from the dinner table where he'd been trying to eat, but stopped when more people spilled into the entryway behind her.

"The airplanes were so cool—"

"I had to sit next to—"

"I saw the Rocky Mountains—"

"Who's here?" Regan said, turning in her seat.

Storm entered the dining room, her face pale. She looked tired and vulnerable, and she'd obviously been crying. Zane's first instinct was to kiss the shadows beneath her eyes away. He steeled himself against any such desires.

"My mother and sisters are here," Storm said in a flat tone, as if she too was beyond the capacity to feel. "I'm sorry. I didn't know they were coming or I would have warned you. Zane, this is Cheyenne. Cheyenne, this is Zane—"

Cheyenne fixed him with an angry look. "Where else were we supposed to go?" she said before he could make up his mind how to greet her. "When you decided to steal my daughter away, you left me high and dry." Her daughters crowded around Storm, who circled them in her arms, but kept her attention on Cheyenne, eyeing the woman like she might set off a bomb at any moment. As far as he was concerned, Storm had already set off a bomb back at Mandy's

Emporium. His future lay in ruins. He didn't need more confusion.

"I… uh… hello." Zane didn't know what else to say. Was this woman in on it too? Did Storm—Kenna—whoever she was—even have a mother? He couldn't remember her ever mentioning one, and hadn't she said she was an only child?

Anger built within him at this new twist. How many lies had Storm set out to tell? Did she really think this new cover-up job could paste over the failed one? How had she even wrangled a fake mother and three sisters in the scant hours since he'd confronted her?

"There's no way I can balance a full-time job with raising three children," Cheyenne went on. "You're selfish to demand it. Of course, you obviously think it's perfectly reasonable to force me from my house, so I suppose I should have expected it."

"I—what the hell is this?" He turned to Storm for an explanation. Storm shook her head helplessly as the girls clamored for her attention.

"Zane—I'm sorry. About everything."

He wanted to block out her words and her pleading expression. Every instinct he had made him want to sweep her into his arms and away from all the chaos, but how could he do that when she'd caused all of it?

Not all of it, a little voice in his head said. He was the one who'd advertised for a fake wife.

That was different, though. He hadn't set out to make Storm love him, knowing all the while he meant to leave her at the end.

Before he could say a word, Cheyenne whirled to face Storm. "I knew it," she said. "You didn't tell him anything, did you? All that baloney about marrying him for real. You were lying! There's no reason you can't get your bonus and come home."

"Mom!"

Zane caught the looks passing between his brothers and their wives. The situation was about to get out of hand. "That's enough," he said loudly. "Everybody, sit down and shut up." His military experience kicked in and he assessed the situation automatically. Goal—information. As much as possible. Priorities—get people fed and talking. There was no need for shouting and dramatics. The game Storm was playing was over, no matter who was the one who'd started it—even Storm must know that.

"I bet these girls are tired and hungry." He hoped his tone made it clear that he expected everyone to settle down. With a look to her husband, Regan stood up and began to shift the chairs to make room for their unexpected guests. Mason went to get a couple more chairs from the kitchen. The girls plunked down on the vacant seats happily while Ella poured glasses of milk. Storm began to ladle food onto the plates Regan fetched. Only Zane and Cheyenne remained standing.

"I'm not eating until Storm comes to her senses and—"

"Then don't eat." Zane cut across her words and jabbed a finger at an empty chair. Cheyenne opened her mouth, closed it. Sat down.

"You still haven't said anything about my hair, Storm," Zoe cried suddenly. "Didn't you notice? I cut it short!"

Zane blessed her for the change of subject. Regan and Ella immediately exclaimed over her hairdo, clearly glad to diffuse the tension in the room.

Storm sent him a grateful look he tried to ignore. He was not on her side. He wouldn't be taken in by her again.

"The twins need haircuts soon, too," Cheyenne suddenly said to Storm in a conversational tone. "I hope there's someone good in town."

"I know an excellent hairdresser," Regan assured her.

Cheyenne looked at the plates of food Regan and Ella were preparing. "Maybe I'm a tiny bit hungry after all."

Zane sat down in his own chair with a thump. How was he ever going to straighten this out?

STORM COULDN'T BELIEVE her mother had chosen this disastrous moment to arrive, and she said a silent prayer of thanks that everyone was now doing their best to smooth things over. As for Zane, he still looked as furious as he'd been when he walked out of Mandy's, but as she watched, he sat down heavily, took a deep breath, got himself under control and bent to look at Zoe's hair.

"You look like a princess, sweetheart."

Storm's heart melted. That was exactly why she'd

fallen for Zane. Only a special man could be kind to a little girl in the midst of all this turmoil.

Austin was sitting next to him. Violet looked from one to the other. "You're twins, just like us!"

"That's right," Austin said to her. "You and your sister and Zane and I are the twin brigade."

"Hear that, Storm? I'm in the twin brigade." Violet beamed at her.

"So you are. I guess I feel left out," Storm made herself say in an even tone. She was close to breaking down, though. Everything was falling apart. She was losing Zane even as she sat here conversing as if nothing was wrong. Not only Zane—all the residents of Crescent Hall. She didn't think she could stand that.

"You have to be left out. You don't have a twin."

"I'm glad *I* don't have a twin," Zoe asserted.

Storm intervened before they started fighting. Whether or not twins were superior to singles was a constant source of contention in her family's home. "Eat your vegetables, Zoe. You, too, Daisy."

"I'm not hungry for vegetables," Daisy said.

"Eat them anyway," Regan said, "and then we'll have dessert."

"Are you our aunt?" Zoe said to her.

"I don't see why not," Regan said. "Auntie Regan. I like the sound of that."

"I'm your Auntie Ella," Ella put in.

Storm swallowed down a fresh wave of sadness at how eagerly Regan and Ella took on their new roles. They wouldn't be her sisters' aunts for long the way things were going. Still, she was grateful at how hard they were all working to pretend this was a normal dinner and not upset the girls. Austin kept up a running conversation with Violet about twins. Zane pestered Daisy until she'd eaten up every green bean on her plate. Mason was smiling at them all from the head of the table as if he couldn't be happier.

But tension framed the gathering, and it didn't bode well for what would come later.

Violet yawned widely, and Daisy yawned after her.

"Looks like it's getting close to bedtime," Regan said. "How about I take you girls upstairs to get ready while your mother relaxes a little? I'll make up rooms for everyone on the third floor. The girls can take the old nursery and you can have a room to yourself, Cheyenne."

"Okay!" Zoe pushed her chair back and hopped up. So did the other girls. A moment later their footsteps were clattering up the stairs.

"Would you like me to go up with you, Mom?" Storm asked, eager to get away from Zane, who had now turned his gaze on her and was studying her, his expression unreadable.

Cheyenne nodded slowly.

Storm followed her up the two flights of stairs, getting more worried about her mother with each step. It wasn't like Cheyenne to be so quiet, or so docile.

"You all right, Mom?" she asked reluctantly when they reached Cheyenne's third floor room, fearing another outburst.

"I'm not used to being told to shut up."

"It's been a hard day around here."

"It's been a hard day for me, too. I'm the one losing my home." Cheyenne's tone was stiff, but she kissed Storm's cheek before going into the room where Regan was finishing making up a bed.

I'm the one losing the man I love, Storm wanted to retort, but that conversation would have to wait for later, when they didn't have an audience.

"Let me know if you need anything," Regan said, slipping out of the room, and heading down the hall toward a larger one at the end where they could hear the girls laughing.

"I hope you sleep well, Mom. We'll talk about everything tomorrow, okay?"

Cheyenne was already closing the door. Storm stood in the hall for a moment, unwilling to leave her mother alone, but unsure what to do. Cheyenne's outburst when she first arrived must have been bravado. If she'd left home it meant she didn't feel like she could pay her bills anymore. Guilt held Storm in place. She had blown everything. She wouldn't get her bonus now, and she wouldn't get Zane either. When she heard her mother's sobs begin, she turned and fled.

Zane was waiting for Storm in her bedroom when she reached it. For a brief moment, she considered walking right back out again, but there was no use postponing this confrontation.

"We'd better talk, don't you think?" he said.

She nodded wearily and shut the door. Whatever he

had to say to her, it was going to be bad. All she could do was endure it. He gestured that she should take a seat, but she shook her head and stayed where she was.

"Want to tell me who you really are?"

She winced and bowed her head. So, the game was up. No wonder he was so angry. She allowed herself one last moment to belong here to Crescent Hall, to Chance Creek and to Zane. She knew when she was done with her explanation, she wouldn't belong to any of them.

"My name is Storm Willow."

CHAPTER SIXTEEN

"**M**Y NAME IS Storm Willow."

Zane swallowed past a lump of pain that threatened to block his throat. She had lied to him right from the start. "Want to tell me why you're pretending to be Kenna North?" His voice was calm, but inside he was struggling to control his temper. He'd always been proud of the way he could keep his cool when times got rough, but the day's events were fast eroding that ability.

"Kenna's my boss. Everything you know about her is true," she rushed on, as if needing to say all of it now that she'd started. "She's the one who arranged the marriage with you."

"Then why are you here?"

"Because she got invited on another climb. She didn't want to miss it."

He let out a disbelieving laugh. Heloise was right, after all. "So she sent you in her place?"

"That's about the size of it. Kenna's like that—practical to a fault."

"Where'd you get the identification?"

"She sent it to me." With every answer, her voice was growing quieter.

"Are you in the habit of doing everything she tells you to do?"

Her head snapped up. "Yes. That's exactly right. I do everything Kenna says, because I don't have a choice!"

"Why the hell not?"

"Because of those three girls up there." She pointed to the ceiling. "Because of my mother, who won't let go of the house my father bought for her, just like you and your brothers won't let go of this ranch. Kenna pays my salary—she offered me a bonus to take her place. You have no right to judge me. You'd do anything for this piece of land—including marrying a stranger. Don't tell me that your ruse to get a fake wife is any better than me stepping into Kenna's shoes to take on her identity." Her chest heaved with indignation. "If you saw my home, you'd understand why my mom won't give it up, even though it's bankrupting all of us. It's special. It's beautiful. It's the most precious gift my father ever gave my mother. So, yes—I will do whatever Kenna says if it means I can keep earning my paycheck. At least, I used to. Not anymore."

"Oh, yeah? What's changed?" he challenged her, even as her words cut him to the quick. She was right; he had been willing to marry a stranger to protect his inheritance. He couldn't defend himself against that accusation.

"I met you." She let that sink in. "I realized that

bankruptcy was better than living a lie. I decided that you were too important to me to give up just because Kenna demanded it. I told Cheyenne the last time we talked on the phone that I wouldn't go through with the ruse—that I was going to tell you who I really was—and that there would be no bonus from Kenna. That's why she's here. She's trying to save her house."

"And I suppose you told Kenna about your change of heart?" He wanted so much to believe her, but he couldn't. She'd lied to him about everything. How could he ever believe her again?

"No. Not yet. I wanted to tell you first."

"So you say now."

She flinched as if he'd struck her. "It's true."

"Do you even know the meaning of that word?"

"Yes, I do. I know I should have told you about Belinda," she said. "I should have told you about me. It all got so complicated so fast."

"That's not good enough. You deliberately made my marriage a lie. I'm going to lose my ranch!"

"Your marriage was going to be a lie no matter what I did!" Her voice rose. "If everything had worked, I would have left after Thanksgiving, you would have inherited this place, and you would never be any the wiser. What would it have mattered if Kenna was here or I was?"

"It just does."

"Fine."

"Fine? What does that mean?"

She rushed to the closet, pulled out her suitcase and

threw it on the bed next to him. She pulled open a dresser drawer and swept her clothes into her arms. "It means I'm leaving."

"You can't do that." He leaned over and grabbed her hand, preventing her from gathering any more of her things. "You made promises to me. You're my wife, damn it."

She stared at him. "Am I? Or is Kenna?"

He nearly growled in frustration. "You're the one who set this in motion, so you're going to see it through. Do you understand me? You're going to get your mother in line, and you're going to ensure that my brothers and I inherit this ranch."

"And if I don't?"

"I'll march you down to the jail myself for fraud and impersonation. And I'll press charges against Cheyenne, too, for aiding and abetting."

"There's no way—"

"Watch me."

Storm blinked at the fury in his words. He watched it sink in that he wasn't fooling around. When she spoke again, her voice was unsteady.

"You want me to act like nothing's changed?"

"That's exactly it. We'll think of something to appease Heloise."

She pressed her lips together. "Fine, I'll do it. Because no matter what you think, when I give my word, I follow through."

Zane stood up, crossed to the closet, pulled out an arm-load of his clothes and dumped them in Storm's suitcase.

"What are you doing?" she asked.

"Moving out."

"Jail?" Cheyenne said early the next morning, staring at her in disbelief.

"Yes—jail," Storm reiterated and stopped pacing around her mother's bedroom. She'd explained everything to Cheyenne from the moment she'd received Kenna's phone call in the motel room to the blowup with Zane the previous night. "Which is why you're going to stop trying to push your agenda and start to help me fix this."

"I don't see how it can be fixed. You've made a real mess of everything."

"Really? I've made the mess? I'm not the one hanging onto a house I can't afford!"

Cheyenne drew back. "What's that got to do with it?"

"Everything! Why was I so desperate to earn that bonus? Why did I agree to this stupid farce to begin with? Because I wanted to help you pay your bills!"

Cheyenne's face went slack. "I never asked you to lie!"

"You didn't stop me either. Worse, you've made damn sure I've *always* known that losing the house would be a disaster you couldn't survive. Which means I've made every decision based on helping you to keep it. I've given up too much of my life to pay that mortgage. I'll have to give up the rest of my life to keep on paying it!"

"I never knew you felt that way."

"Now you do!"

They stared at each other, both of them breathing hard. Cheyenne's face crumpled. "I didn't mean to ruin everything. I just... I just miss Mitch so much. I miss having a husband. I want my family back—my life back."

Storm paced away. "The thing is, Mom—you can't have him back. All you can do is move forward." She was speaking to herself as much as her mother. Her own heart felt torn in two by the thought of leaving Crescent Hall—of leaving Zane. She'd be jobless—homeless—possibly pregnant. She'd have to start all over again.

But there was no crying over spilt milk. No way to pick up the pieces or turn back time. All she could do—all any of them could do—was go on the best they could. Maybe if she'd spoken her mind to her mother a long time ago, neither of them would be in their current predicament. It was time to put away sentiment and think with clear heads.

Cheyenne sat down on the bed, buried her face in her hands and began to cry. Storm crossed the room and knelt in front of her.

"We have to sell the house," she said quietly. After a long moment, Cheyenne nodded.

"I miss him, too, you know," Storm whispered.

"I know, honey."

Storm rested her head on her mother's lap, and

finally let her own tears come.

"THIS ISN'T WORKING," Mason said a few days later. "You and Storm couldn't fool a blind man that you're in love. Even Storm's sisters know something's wrong."

Zane knew what he meant. The two of them had barely spoken. Storm edged through the halls like a ghost when she was home, spending most of her time on the third floor with her mother and sisters. Other times a taxi came and carried them all off to town, presumably to work in the store. When they came back at meal times the Willows joined the rest of the family, and both Storm and Cheyenne did their best to make conversation, but those meals were quiet affairs—far different from the rowdy, loud ones they'd shared only days before.

"How are you going to convince Heloise that you're marrying Storm for real? She knows she's not Kenna, right? What's the plan?"

"I don't have one."

"Hell." Mason walked away. Came back. "Storm has to talk to her. She has to admit that she lied about her identity, but that she really loves you."

"I can't ask her to do that now."

"Like hell you can't."

"Maybe I should send her away. Start over."

"You know what? Maybe you should."

Zane rounded on him. "Fuck off!"

Mason laughed. "Yeah, just like I thought. You

love her, Zane. No matter that she lied to you about who she is. No matter that she got one over on you. You love her. Why don't you start from there?"

"What the hell does that mean?"

"Make her love you back. For real. Get this disaster back on rails."

Zane watched him leave, his mind trying to make sense of what Mason had said. Make Storm love him? How? And how would he know if her love was real?

It was a stupid idea.

But a compelling one nonetheless. Mason was right; he did love Storm despite everything. Maybe he was a fool, but he was a fool who knew exactly what he wanted.

And what Gunnery Sergeant Zane Hall wants, Gunnery Sergeant Zane Hall gets.

Damn straight. Zane squared his shoulders. Why shouldn't he walk out of this disaster with the wife he wanted, kids on the way and the deed to Crescent Hall in his hand? He wasn't a quitter. He'd faced tougher challenges than this and succeeded.

And he knew just where to start.

STORM WAS FOLDING shirts the following afternoon when a knock came at the door of Mandy's. Her first response was dismay. What new nightmare was fate serving up? When Zane gathered his things and moved to a bedroom down the hall the night Cheyenne had arrived, it had broken her heart. It wasn't until he walked out her door that she'd fully realized their relationship was over. There was no fixing this—not now that he knew how deeply her lies had run. No trace of tenderness toward her was left in him.

They'd spent the intervening days avoiding each other, or pretending nothing was wrong at all when the girls were present. Storm was still avoiding Mia's phone calls. There was no way she could face the wedding planner now. Cheyenne was a changed woman, silently moving through the Hall, helping where she could, staying out of the way otherwise. Storm knew she had listed the cottage with a real estate agent and was trying to drum up the courage to return to California to begin packing. She hadn't made a reservation for a return flight, however, and Storm knew she was having a hard time facing the future.

Often Cheyenne and the girls accompanied her to the store, but today her mother had begged off with a headache and Regan had said she'd watch the girls. They'd been cooped up too long indoors and could use a day outside exploring the ranch. Storm was grateful for the time alone.

When she opened the door, Zane stood outside, Belinda beside him. Storm was so surprised she couldn't speak for a moment, but then she ushered them in. What did it mean that Zane would make this gesture? He'd been so sure she was in league with Darren, and that Belinda was in on a trick meant to do him harm. Storm had told him how wrong he was about that. Was he trying to issue an apology?

"I'm so glad to see you," she said to Belinda.

"I'm glad to be here." She scanned the store. "What should I do first?"

"I'll leave you two to your work," Zane said, turning away.

"Thank you," Storm said, following him outside before he could disappear. "It means a lot to me that you would speak to Belinda." She didn't want to let him go. She was afraid if she did, they'd go back to avoiding each other and she'd missed him bitterly these last few days.

"I was wrong about her." He settled his hat on his head. "She and Darren had nothing to do with your trick."

Sorrow rippled through her at the way he phrased that. He was obviously still angry. She didn't think that would ever change. Still, she needed to try to make him understand.

"Zane."

He waited, expressionless, for her to go on.

"It's true; I did what I did at first to get the bonus Kenna promised me. I did need the money. But the minute I met you I wanted you." She took a deep breath, searching for the courage to go on. "I knew right away I'd been given an incredible chance. I'd never met someone like you before. I really did fall in love."

A muscle twitched in his jaw. "I wish to God I could believe that."

She took in his rigid stance. "You can believe me. Zane, you're motivated by the same things I am—love for your family and a desire for a better future. I didn't pretend to be Kenna to hurt you. I did it to help my mother and sisters. Now they're here and Mom's decided to sell our house. There's no reason for me to lie anymore."

"Prove it."

"How? What can I possibly do except stay right here and keep telling you?" she asked in exasperation.

"You could show me."

His words were so quiet at first she thought she'd heard him wrong. "Show you?"

He nodded.

Did he mean—?

She didn't stop to analyze it. She stepped closer, went up on tiptoes and planted a kiss at the corner of his mouth. "Like that?"

"Something like that."

His tone was still stern, still uncompromising, but Storm felt a ray of hope.

She kissed him again, splaying her fingers over his chest to brace herself as she reached up to brush her lips over his cheek.

"You're getting colder," he said wryly.

"Sorry." She tried again, this time kissing him square on the mouth. At first he held still and it was like kissing a statue, his lips hard and unyielding. Then his arms wrapped around her and he kissed her back, pulling her closer and deepening the kiss with a groan.

Tears pricked Storm's eyes as she clung to him, so hungry for his touch she couldn't get enough.

"Get a room!" some wag in a beat-up Ford called out as he drove by. Zane broke off the embrace, looking around him as if he'd forgotten where he was.

"That's not the worst idea," he said finally.

Storm nearly laughed with relief. He could joke about it. "You're insatiable." She was so grateful for that.

"Like you aren't," Zane said, his hands tracing her hips.

"Zane—what does this mean?" She had to know, as much as she didn't want to break the spell of this moment.

"I guess it means I'm too dumb to quit." He kissed her again.

"You mean it—you'll give me another chance?"

He looked at her. "What choice do I have? I know any sane man would walk away, but I can't seem to do that. Maybe that means I'm crazy."

"A good kind of crazy."

"What about you?" He framed her face with his hands. "Are you willing to give us another chance? A real chance?"

She nodded. "Of course. I love you, Zane."

He crushed her to him. "Thank God. I love you, too."

CHAPTER SEVENTEEN

"**W**HAT KIND OF a mission keeps a man out of contact for four or five months?" Austin was saying when Zane joined his brothers in the stables the next morning. He was due to bring Cheyenne and the girls to town to meet Storm for lunch at a local restaurant later, but now he had to catch up on his chores. He'd slept late after an unforgettable night of lovemaking with Storm. It was as if both of them had needed to make up for lost time. Waking up beside her was the sweetest reward for patching thing up between them.

"It's barely been one month," Mason said.

"Yeah, but he said we wouldn't hear from him until Christmas time. That's a hell of a long time."

"Talking about Colt?" Zane asked, moving to the stall where Jasper poked his nose over the door, snuffling Zane's hand when he reached up to stroke him.

"Don't you think it's strange?" Austin challenged him.

"A little. I figure he's on the kind of mission that

takes time to set into place."

"Like what?"

Zane shrugged. "Guess we'll find out when he comes back."

"If—" Austin broke off as his brothers turned on him. "Sorry." He raised his hands in an apologetic gesture. "We're all thinking it."

"I'm thinking that Colt's one of the best combat controllers the Air Force has ever seen. He'll get the job done and get home as soon as he can," Mason said.

"You're right." Austin ducked his head. "I shouldn't have said it. I'm going to get back to work."

Zane found it hard to shake his worry even without Austin there to give voice to his fears. When he'd been in the Marines he hadn't had time to think much about his brothers; he'd been too busy keeping himself alive. Now that he was home it was another matter. Back on the ranch, it only seemed right that the family would be reunited. Colt should be here, too.

He'd have to get used to him being away, though. Even when this mission was over, there would be others, if Colt had his way.

"Is it my imagination or are things on the mend between you and Storm?" Mason asked.

"We've made progress."

"You need to talk to Heloise. We can't put her off any longer."

Zane sighed. "You're right. I'll talk to Storm first, though. See what we can come up with."

"A lot's riding on this."

"You think I don't know that?"

Mason put his hands up in a placating manner. "I'm sure you do. I'm just reminding you. Tell Heloise the truth, not some trumped up story."

Zane didn't want to think about how that would go. "Like I said, we'll see what we can come up with."

His brother hesitated. "When I think about losing all of this again…"

Zane clapped him on the shoulder. "Stop that thought right there. I'm not going to let you down."

WHEN STORM ANSWERED her phone later that morning, Heloise launched an immediate attack.

"I didn't think I was handing you a hobby when I gave you Mandy's," she said. "I thought you had gumption in you. Maybe you're afraid of a little hard work."

"I'm not afraid of work, Heloise." Storm stayed calm. "I'm working right now. I've been here almost every day, and my mother and sisters arrived in town recently."

"And you haven't brought them to see me?"

"They've barely gotten settled in." Storm thought fast. She could almost hear Heloise working herself into a tizzy. "I'll bring them today, though. How's that? In an hour or so?" Zane was due to bring them by the store soon.

"Well… fine. Do that. While you're at it you can explain how you've cloned yourself. It's a neat trick to be climbing a mountain in Nepal and renovating a store at the same time." Heloise hung up.

Storm stared at the phone in horror as she realized Heloise must have been the one who'd spilled the beans about her to Zane. If Heloise knew she was a fake, then the whole ranch was in jeopardy. No wonder Zane had lost his cool. At the time she'd thought it was the lies that had angered him, and she hadn't blamed him one bit, but if Heloise knew she wasn't Kenna, then she must have guessed their upcoming wedding was a fake.

"What's wrong?" Zane said, coming into Mandy's. Her mother and sisters followed close behind him. Zane took Storm's arm and led her to a corner of the store where they could talk alone.

"That was Heloise. She knows. You never told me!"

"She looked Kenna up on the Internet. Old girl's smarter than me." He dropped a kiss on her head to take the sting from the words. "We need to talk about that, though. If we're going to go through with the wedding, we need to go see her and admit that you've been impersonating Kenna. See if we can convince her that's the only lie, though."

"The ranch—" she said faintly.

"Is going to be just fine when you tell Heloise that you were acting as Kenna in order to make money, but you fell in love with me along the way."

"You want me to tell her the truth?"

"That much of it."

"But—" She scrambled to sort it all out. "She

knows you tried to hire a fake bride."

"That's right. We come clean and confess every-thing. Then we hope she gives us a second chance."

"She won't believe that we love each other now! She'll take Crescent Hall away!"

"What else can we do?"

"I don't know." She looked at him helplessly. "I'm so sorry, Zane."

"I had it coming, I guess. Should have known not to ever try to fool her. You'd better think it through, though. If you marry me, and Heloise refuses to hold up her end of the bargain, we won't have a home. I won't have a livelihood. We'll have to start over."

"I don't care about that," she said. "I care about you. All of you. This is your home."

"This is your home, too. Let's go fight for it."

IT WAS A subdued group that Zane shepherded to the assisted living center fifteen minutes later. Even Zoe, Daisy and Violet had been told that this was a serious visit and that they had to be on their best behavior. When Heloise let them into her apartment, she looked the newcomers over, and gestured for them to take seats on the sofa.

"Mrs. *Willow*, I take it," she said to Cheyenne.

Cheyenne cast a glance at Storm. "Yes. That's right."

"These are all your daughters?"

"Yes."

"Why so many years between Storm and her sisters?"

Cheyenne frowned at the personal question. Zane intervened. "Heloise."

"I'm curious. Maybe it explains Storm's behavior," Heloise said sharply.

Color rose on Cheyenne's cheeks. "Mitch and I didn't mean to start our family so young, but when we found out I was pregnant with Storm we got married and never regretted it. Once my husband got his surfing sponsorship, we went on to have more children. That has nothing to do with the way Storm—"

"I see." Heloise cut her off and sat down on the love seat across from them. She turned to Storm. "Your turn. I hear you have something to say."

"I do. I'll keep it brief." She didn't look happy and Zane knew she would have preferred that her sisters didn't hear what she had to say. "My boss, Kenna North, offered me a cash bonus to take on her persona for six weeks while she was out of the country. I said yes."

"No matter that you were committing fraud and helping to swindle an old woman out of her property?"

"Oh, come on, Heloise," Zane said. "You're not blameless here. You've set impossible conditions on us inheriting that property. We're doing the best we can."

"Including hiring women to act as your wife?"

"One woman, and I didn't hire her. Kenna needed a husband, I needed a wife. It was a trade."

"But you got Storm, instead."

"That's right, and that made it a lot more compli-cated, because I fell in love with her. Not just a temporary love, not just a convenient love, but gut-wrenching, in-your-face, forever love. I'm going to marry Storm. Whatever you pull next, she's going to be my wife. We'll leave Chance Creek if we have to, but we'll leave it together."

"I see." Heloise picked up the teapot that sat on a tray on the coffee table and poured a cup. She offered it to Cheyenne. "You're willing to leave Crescent Hall behind, are you?"

Zane nodded, not trusting himself to speak.

"What about your brothers? Are they willing, too?"

"I can't speak for them. You know it'll damn well kill them—"

"But you'll still leave them in the lurch."

"Damn it, Heloise—what do you want from me? You want me to lie? You want me to marry someone else? You want to pull some more strings and watch me dance around like a goddamn puppet? I love her—"

"Calm down." Heloise poured another cup and handed it to Storm who took it with trembling fingers. Tears shone in her eyes and Zane reached the breaking point. He wasn't going to subject his wife to any more—

"I accept Storm as a candidate for your wife. I expect your marriage to continue as planned. I suggest you speak to your wedding planner," she added severely. "The poor girl resorted to calling me since you've all been avoiding her. If you are married in church before your family and friends, under your *real* names," she looked from one to the other, "then I will forget the rest of this travesty and continue on as before."

Zane took a deep breath. "We can do that." A small sound from Storm caught his attention. She sent him a look that told him she needed to speak to him alone. "I need some air. Storm, come with me, would you? Heloise, try to be nice to your guests."

"Of course." Heloise appeared affronted. As Zane headed for the door he heard her say to Cheyenne, "How did you manage to get your hair that color, dear?"

He hurried Storm out of the room. "What's wrong now?"

"Aside from the fact World War III is about to start in there?" She turned to him. "How are you going to get a divorce from Kenna in less than a month?"

STORM TRIED TO keep her mind on the store the next several days instead of falling prey to the dire scenarios her imagination was cooking up. Zane had said he'd take care of Kenna, but she wondered how on earth he planned to do that. For one thing, Kenna was most likely inaccessible. Unless her climb had been disrupted, she'd be somewhere on a mountain, far out of reach of cell phones and lawyers. Other fears assailed her. If lawyers were involved wouldn't the fraud she'd committed be exposed? Would she end up in jail? And what would Kenna do? She'd be furious when she found out her inheritance was in jeopardy.

With Cheyenne and Belinda helping her, she finished preparations for the tag sale more quickly than she'd expected, and decided to go ahead with it. Anything to keep from worrying about the future. They put up flyers everywhere they could think of, and posted a notice on the front door, too. "I wonder if anyone will come?" Storm said when they packed up that night.

At the last minute, Belinda told her she wouldn't be able to help out at the sale. She claimed she had an appointment, but Storm was sure that she still hadn't told Darren about working at the store. If she didn't do so soon, Storm would have to think about hiring someone else, and she didn't want to do that. She'd come to enjoy Belinda's dry sense of humor and enthusiasm.

The following morning she was shocked when she opened the store to find a lineup outside. She was surprised by the outpouring of praise from the shoppers, too.

"We really need a new clothing store in town," a lithe brunette with a darling baby girl told her. "I can't wait to see what you bring in. I'm Autumn Cruz, by the way. I'm a friend of Regan and Ella. I'll be by soon to welcome you to town properly. I heard your mother and sisters have come to stay, too."

"Yes, they have."

Autumn laughed at the confusion Storm felt sure

must be clear on her face. "Everyone knows everything about everyone else in this town," she said. "You've been a topic of conversation for weeks around here. I would have been by earlier, but just when I thought I'd given you enough time to settle in, your family arrived."

"I hope you'll come to visit soon, then," Storm said and she meant it. She wanted to meet more women in town if she was going to stay here.

"I think we can call this a success," Cheyenne said at noon when Storm asked her if she was ready to order some lunch.

"I think we can, too," Storm said. More of the old clothes had disappeared than she'd expected, and she was getting excited at the idea of putting together an order for their replacement. Even the little girls had gotten into the spirit of things and when they held up a shirt or skirt and smiled winsomely, it was hard for the good women of Chance Creek to tell them no. It didn't hurt that Storm had marked everything down so low that it hardly made sense not to buy them. At the end of the day, she wouldn't be rich, but at least there would be room for new stock.

"What would you like to eat? Do you want—?"

She was interrupted by the arrival of Ella and Regan who came in bearing takeout bags and boxes that smelled heavenly.

"Girls—go get those chairs from in back," Cheyenne called. She helped Storm lug out a folding table and set it up near the checkout counter. Regan set the chairs around it. Ella passed around napkins and forks and handed out drinks.

When Storm dug into her pita and hummus, she moaned with appreciation. "This is good."

"Try the falafel," Regan said. "Everything at Fila's is amazing."

They took turns helping the customers and eating until everyone was full. Storm expected Ella and Regan to leave then, but after they packed up the remainder of the food, they stayed to help. Storm set them to work rehanging clothes and fixing the displays that interested customers had put into disarray. She sent the twins to take a walk around the block since they'd been inside all morning, and was about to go have a chat with her mother when she saw that Cheyenne was helping a middle-aged cowboy in jeans and a plaid shirt search through a pile of cotton shirts she'd arranged on a table.

"What size is your niece?" she heard Cheyenne say.

The man hesitated. Pointed to Zoe. "About her size, I'd say."

"We mostly have women's clothes, but there might be one or two things for a girl." Cheyenne lifted up one in pink. "What do you think?"

"Well, uh… I guess so," the cowboy said, scratching the back of his neck. "The truth is, I usually get her a stuffed animal, but my sister says she's too old for that now."

"I don't think you're ever too old for a stuffed animal," Cheyenne declared. "That's like saying you're too old for love!"

The cowboy seemed entranced by this proclamation, and why wouldn't he be, Storm thought. Cheyenne was beautiful when she was happy—willowy and vibrant. Storm wondered why she hadn't married again in the years since her father died. Cheyenne hadn't even dated much. That must have been lonely for her.

Shame coursed through Storm when she realized she had never even considered that before—that after the loss of her husband, Cheyenne had taken herself off the market. Had she wanted to protect her daughters from being hurt again?

"You're right. You're never too old for love," the man said. "My granny got married for the second time at seventy-five. Guess I've got a few years left to find…" He trailed off. "Well, never mind."

Cheyenne fixed him with a look Storm recognized all too well. Her mother loved it when people admitted to having strong feelings. "I won't never mind. What were you going to say?"

"Only that maybe you and me… I'm not sure. I could come and get you…"

"Like a date," Cheyenne said, looking up at him from under her lashes. "Like…dinner, maybe. And dancing?"

The cowboy straightened, a grin spreading over his face. "Well now, you did that far better than I was going to. Saved me a lot of stammering and embarrassment."

"No need for embarrassment. I like plain speaking."

Storm bit back a laugh. Cheyenne hadn't liked it so much when she'd arrived in Chance Creek.

"I like women who like plain speaking," the cowboy said.

"We'll get along just fine, then."

"When do you get off work?"

"Five o'clock."

He lifted his hat and settled it back on his head. "I'll pick you up then."

Storm realized the whole store had gone quiet as this little drama had played out. The minute the cowboy cleared the door, Cheyenne beamed. "I have a date! With a cowboy!"

Laughter rippled through the customers and Storm let out a breath she'd been holding.

"Better watch out—that cowboy will rope your heart," someone called out.

"Oh, my gosh! I don't even know his name." Cheyenne raised a hand to her mouth.

"That's Henry Montlake. Hank, for short," another woman said. "He's a good man. Never been married. Had a serious sweetheart in his twenties, but she broke his heart."

"Don't you break his heart," the first woman said. "If you like plain speaking, then you let him know if he's not the one for you."

Cheyenne looked around at the women in the store and nodded solemnly. "I won't break Hank's heart. I promise." She crossed her heart dramatically. She came over to Storm and took her arm. Storm braced herself for a joke or scathing remark at the women's expense. Cheyenne didn't like to be told what to do. Instead, she said, "Well, what do you think of that? This old lady still has game."

"You're not an old lady." Storm wasn't sure what to make of what had just happened. Her mother dating a cowboy? Having fun helping to run the store?

This was a Cheyenne she'd never met.

CHAPTER EIGHTEEN

"SERIOUSLY? A DATE with Hank Montlake?" Austin asked the next morning when Zane met him on horseback down near the creek.

"That's right. She didn't get back until after midnight," Zane said. "She seemed pretty happy this morning. Humming and singing to herself."

"Really?"

Zane shrugged. He put a soothing hand on his mount. "Yep. I think Hank might have made a good impression on her."

"How about you? Making any progress on how to divorce Kenna?"

"Not much." The trouble was he hadn't known what to do first. Should he contact a lawyer and potentially open a can of worms he couldn't close again due to the legal implications of the fraud Storm had committed? Or should he try to get a message to Kenna on her remote mountaintop and give her the lead time to dig in her heels and refuse to allow the marriage to be annulled? He'd ended up calling the minister who was supposed to officiate at his ceremony, Reverend Joe Halpern. He'd known Halpern since he was a child. Maybe the man would have some advice.

"What's on tap today in the meanwhile?" Austin changed the subject, for which Zane was grateful.

"Riding lessons, soon as everyone's up."

"For Storm?"

"For her whole family. The girls should know how to ride, and if Cheyenne's going to date a cowboy, she'd better learn."

"Guess so."

Zane worried that the girls wouldn't want to try it, but at the first mention of horses when he found Storm, Cheyenne and the girls at their breakfast, all three girls turned to their mother and begged her to say yes to lessons.

Cheyenne turned to him. "Is it safe?"

"Jasper's the gentlest gelding you'll ever meet. I think the girls would enjoy it."

"Okay, I guess that's all right."

Zane ushered the girls out to the nearest corral after they were done eating. He enlisted Austin's help and taught them one at a time, with Jasper a willing participant. The horse seemed to enjoy the attention and stood patiently while they took turns. Zane looked up forty-five minutes later to find Storm had joined Cheyenne in leaning against the high corral fence and watching them. Zoe and Violet were perched on top of the rails beside them. It was Daisy's turn to ride.

"She's a natural," he called out to them. "You

should be proud of her!"

Daisy waved to her mother and sisters, a broad grin on her face.

"You're doing great, Daisy!" Cheyenne called back. "Keep up the good work."

"I love you, Jasper," Daisy cried, and patted the horse's flank.

Even Storm smiled at Daisy's sweet voice. Zane made sure to keep watch over her as she progressed around the ring. When she was done, he lifted her off and brought her back to her mom. "Cheyenne, I think it's your turn next."

At first he thought she would say no, but after a moment's hesitation, she said, "Why not? I've always wondered what it would be like."

"I don't think you can ride in that skirt, Mom," Storm said. "Why don't you run and change. Do you have some pants?"

"Yoga pants," Cheyenne said.

"They'll do," Zane said, not wanting to lose momentum. Cheyenne turned for the house, the two littlest girls following her.

"What about you, Storm?" Zoe said. "Did you learn how to ride already?"

"No. I don't think—"

"You have to! You can't be the only one who doesn't know how."

Zane thanked Zoe silently for doing the job of asking Storm for him. After their first lesson, they'd never quite gotten around to it again.

"The horse is probably getting tired."

"Are you crazy? Look at him. He wants you to ride him. He'll be so sad if you don't," Zoe pleaded with her.

Zane considered turning a puppy dog expression on Storm like Zoe had fixed her with, but on second thought decided he wasn't half so cute and probably couldn't pull it off.

"Oh, fine. Fine. You win!"

Zane wasn't sure if she was talking to him or Zoe. He didn't care. He'd gotten what he'd wanted—another chance to show her how wonderful his world was.

STORM APPROACHED THE tall beast with apprehension. Her last lesson felt like a long time ago now, and Zane had ridden behind her for most of it. Zane helped her on, while Austin steadied Jasper and soon she was just as exhilarated as she'd been the first time.

"It's a gratifying thing to work with an animal," Zane said, catching her eye. "It's pretty special. I think we lost something when we switched to cars. Gained a lot, too, of course."

"Of course." But she knew what he meant. She tried to imagine what it would feel like to harness up a horse each time she went to town. To interact with living creatures each time she needed a ride. Would it make her feel more connected in some way to the natural world?

"Looking good," Cheyenne called out from the

fence.

"I guess it's my mom's turn." She sounded wistful even to her own ears.

"Don't worry. I'll give you more lessons any time you want one. Pretty soon you'll be an expert at it."

She found herself smiling back at the handsome cowboy, and when he lifted her down, she was all too aware of him—his muscular arms, broad chest and powerful shoulders. He held her a moment longer than necessary once her feet touched solid ground. Could he tell she wished he would kiss her?

His hands tightened on her waist and he bent down to brush his lips over hers. It was too brief for her to hold onto the sensation but she tried to anyhow. She wanted to hold onto everything that happened to her these days. She was so afraid her time here at Crescent Hall was running out, despite the promises they'd made to each other.

"Oooh, Zane and Storm are kissing!" Zoe crowed from the fence.

"Zane and Storm are allowed to kiss. They'll be husband and wife soon," Cheyenne said.

Husband and wife. If only she was right. Her first marriage to Zane meant nothing in the eyes of the law, and they didn't know if they'd be able to marry a second time before Heloise's deadline was up. For that to happen, Kenna was going to have to cooperate, and who even knew where Kenna was now?

Zane's hands tightened on her waist. "We'll figure it out," he said in a low tone.

"Promise?" She leaned against him, basking in his strength and solidity.

"I promise."

"HI, ZANE!"

Zane turned around at Richard's greeting to find that his nephew had climbed up on the fence a few feet away from Zoe. "Hi, Richard. Good to see you. Come to get a riding lesson?"

"I already know how to ride." His nephew's disgust was plain.

"Just teasing." Zane exchanged a good-natured grin with the boy. "Have you met our guests?"

Richard shook his head.

"This is Cheyenne Willow, Storm's mother."

Cheyenne looked askance at Richard. "I guess that makes you my grand-nephew. Don't you dare call me Great Aunt Cheyenne, though. You can call me Auntie, or just plain Cheyenne."

"Why don't you want to be called Great?"

Cheyenne shuddered theatrically. "I'm not nearly old enough to be called that. Storm, tell him."

"Call her Great Aunt just to make her mad," Storm advised him.

Richard cocked his head. "I'll call you Auntie." His gaze turned to the three girls.

"These are my sisters, Zoe, Violet and Daisy." Storm pointed at each one in turn.

"Hi." Now Richard seemed shy, but Zoe was anything but.

"Hi! I like your boots. Are you good at riding? I just rode for the first time."

Zane liked the way Richard sat up a little taller. "I've been riding for years."

"Cool. How old are you?"

"Twelve."

"I'm eleven." Zoe beamed at him. "Can you show us the ranch?"

Violet hopped off the fence. "I want to see the creek."

Richard looked to him for permission.

"Sure, take them to the creek," Zane said, "but everyone needs to stay back from the water's edge. It's too cold for swimming. You older ones watch the younger ones."

"I'll keep them safe," Richard said, already leading the way.

"You're twice as tall as me," Violet was saying when they reached the track to the creek. All the adults laughed.

"She's right. You grow them tall around here," Cheyenne said.

"That's the Hall genes. Well, Cheyenne, you ready for your ride?"

"You bet."

"THE GIRLS SURE do love it here."

Storm looked up from reading the manual that had come with her new cash register at the shop a week later to find Cheyenne had come in without her even hearing her. "I left them on the ranch with Zane and Richard. Another riding lesson," Cheyenne explained.

Storm nodded and lifted a hand to her temple. She hadn't felt right since she'd gotten up this morning, but she hated to take even a day off from prepping the store. "They can't get enough of those riding lessons." The girls' enthusiasm had spurred Storm to take it more seriously than she would have if they hadn't been here. It tickled her to find out that sibling rivalry was alive and well between them. The thought that her younger sisters might outstrip her at riding made her a strong student, and Zane had noticed that. He had teased her about it the night before when they met in their room before dinner, but kissed her to show that he didn't really mean it. Storm had enjoyed that kiss as much as all the others. Cheyenne and the girls had all settled in as if they'd always lived here. Storm was beginning to feel that way herself. She could predict the patterns and whereabouts of everyone in the family, and she'd grown accustomed to all the new sounds and smells of the ranch so that she hardly noticed them anymore.

"They love more than the horses," Cheyenne said. "They love the company."

"You mean Richard?"

"Richard is only part of it." Cheyenne moved around the empty store. The back room was piled with merchandise and metal racks. Storm had decided that the renovation trumped everything else that needed to be done with the store. "I think they love having all those men around. Zane, Austin, Mason—they love the security and the playfulness."

Storm thought that over. She recalled Zane's careful coaching of the girls when they rode. She thought about the way Mason and Regan cracked jokes throughout the meals until the girls couldn't eat for their giggling. Austin had been more than happy to race against Zane on the obstacle course again and again and again so the girls could time them with a stopwatch.

The men did all kinds of things that she and her mother had never thought to do with the girls. They roughhoused and pretend-wrestled. They taught them how to throw a baseball and got up impromptu games of soccer in the wide backyard. They'd even taken them fishing.

Zoe, Violet and Daisy were going to miss all of that when they went home. Storm would miss them, too. She'd come to love the noisy meals and the easy camaraderie among all of them. She couldn't bear the thought that if Kenna refused to divorce Zane, they all might have to leave Crescent Hall.

She shivered against a sudden wash of cold down her spine. For some reason she hadn't been able to get warm all morning. "How was your date last night?" she asked.

"Fun." Her mother smiled. "We went dancing again."

"Since when do you know how to dance to country music?" Maybe she should just give up and go home now, but she'd wanted to get the cash register working today. She should put in another hour.

Cheyenne shrugged. "Dancing is dancing. Especially with a handsome man."

Storm peered at her mother. "Are you falling in love with that cowboy?"

Cheyenne turned away. "Love seems like too strong a word. I certainly like him a lot, though."

But Storm knew her mother too well to buy that. "You *are* falling in love with him. Mom!"

"I didn't plan it." Cheyenne lifted her hands helplessly. "Me and a cowboy? It's ridiculous."

A wave of vertigo rolled through Storm and she gripped the counter to keep her balance. She wasn't going to get the register running at this rate. Time to call it a day and go home and rest. "It's not ridiculous. It's just... inconvenient. Does he know you'll be heading back home at some point?" She closed the manual and put it underneath the counter.

"He knows I live in California, yes. But—" She hesitated a moment. "I'm beginning to think that maybe I should stay in Chance Creek. The girls hate to be separated from you," she went on in a rush before Storm could speak, "and so do I."

"We might not be staying here all that long if Zane can't get his marriage to Kenna annulled."

"Even if Heloise kicks you all off the ranch, which I can't believe she'd do," Cheyenne said, "would you leave the area? Seems to me everyone loves it here. There must be other ranches."

"You know the cost of things. Even pooling every-one's money together, I don't think we could buy anything like Crescent Hall."

"Maybe you could if your mother kicked in the proceeds from selling her ridiculously priced beach house," Cheyenne mused.

Storm could only stare at her. "Mom?"

"I got an offer this morning. Two point five mil-lion. After paying the balance of the mortgage, that's still well over a million dollars left. My accountant says I have to sink it into something or I'll lose too much to capital gains!"

"You'd buy a ranch—for me?"

"And for me, and for your sisters and the rest of those hangers-on you've accumulated." Cheyenne waved a hand to include everyone on the ranch.

Tears pricked Storm's eyes. She'd never expected Cheyenne to do such a thing.

"Hey, none of that. I'm trying to make you happy!"

"I am happy! Are you sure, Mom? You love that house."

"No. I loved Mitch and the fact he gave it to me. I love you, too, and Zoe and Daisy and Violet, and you're the ones that need a real home. I think we've found that here, if you don't mind your cranky old mother living in a little cabin on the far corner of the property. Don't want to cramp your style."

"As if you could." Storm threw her arms around her mother, and danced her around the room.

"Come on, let's celebrate. I'll call Hank and tell him

to meet us at Fila's in fifteen minutes. I want a big bowl of curry and some naan."

The mention of food—spicy foreign food, at that—pushed Storm over the edge. Clapping a hand to her mouth, she raced for the bathroom and got there just in time. She was sick until her throat felt raw.

"Storm? Are you all right?"

"Ugh, I feel awful. I don't know what's wrong with me." Flushing the toilet she washed her hands and splashed cold water on her face. At least she was feeling a little better now.

"Really? You don't know what's wrong?" Cheyenne asked, arching an eyebrow. "Could it possibly be you've been having too much fun with your own cowboy?"

Storm braced herself on the counter as the truth dawned on her.

She must be pregnant.

CHAPTER NINETEEN

W HEN ZANE ARRIVED home from his meeting
with Reverend Halpern, he found Regan and
Cheyenne in the kitchen with the girls.

"Storm's in her room," Cheyenne said before he
even asked. "She'll want you to look in on her."

"Okay. Is something up?" He didn't trust the way
the women were exchanging glances, but he decided to
go right to the source to get his answer. He made his
way upstairs and let himself into the bedroom, where
he was surprised to find Storm tucked in bed, pale and
drawn. "Hey, what's wrong?"

"Just a little under the weather."

He sat down on the edge of her bed and put his
hand to her forehead.

"I don't have a fever; it's something else."

"What?"

She squeezed his hand with hers, then reached
under the covers. When she pulled it back out, she
waved a pink plastic indicator at him. "I'm pregnant,"
she whispered.

For a moment, Zane couldn't breathe. He couldn't

think, either. "Pregnant?"

"Pregnant."

"You're pregnant?"

She nodded. "What do you think?"

He climbed right onto the bed and crouched over her. "I think you're brilliant!"

"You're not angry?"

"Why would I be angry?" He planted a kiss on her forehead, then her chin. Then her nose.

"Because we don't know what's going to happen next."

Zane reared back. "I know exactly what's going to happen next. We're going to get married. We're going to spend the rest of our lives together. We're going to raise this child among the people we love."

"But—"

"But nothing. That's how it's going to be. You're mine forever, Storm Willow. We pledged that once already, remember? We're going to pledge it again." A grin spread over his face. "At our shotgun wedding." He lifted her hands in his. "Pregnant!" He kissed her again.

"There's something else. Cheyenne plans to stay in Chance Creek."

"I'm glad to hear that."

Storm smiled. "I'm glad to hear that you're glad to hear it, because she has some pretty good news, too."

Zane sat down. "Don't tell me she's pregnant—"

"No! Heck, I hadn't thought of that." Storm shook the disturbing idea off. "No, she got an offer on the beach house and she took it. She made a lot of money." She tugged at Zane's hands. "Don't get mad—I know we'll figure out a way to save Crescent Hall, but if we don't—"

"Don't talk like that."

"If we don't," she pressed on, "Cheyenne's going to buy a ranch. A place for all of us to be together. So we'll keep figuring out how to get to Kenna, and how to make Heloise happy, but we have a backup plan just in case."

He thought about that. Realized as much as it riled him to think about losing, he couldn't feel anything but grateful to have a fallback position.

"Cheyenne's fallen hard for Hank," was all he said.

Storm's smile told him she understood that was as far as he could take things. "Yes, I figured that out today."

"She could do a lot worse."

"She sure could." She tugged at his hands. "What did the minister say?"

"Well, he thinks the marriage can be annulled since I never actually met Kenna, and she didn't speak the vows or sign the paperwork. The difficult part is the fraud aspect. Halpern's no lawyer. He doesn't know what to think, but it seems likely if the marriage is annulled and Kenna doesn't press charges, nothing will happen."

"But we need Kenna."

"We need Kenna. I think it's time to try to contact her." He let go of her hands. "I even looked into flying to Nepal and going after her myself, but that would take too long. I'd never catch her in time."

"I'm sorry."

"So am I. But you know what?"

"What?"

"We're going to be okay, no matter what. All of us are."

"I know."

He thought a minute. "I'll tell you what else."

"What?"

"First thing tomorrow, we're going to go buy a ring. And we'll talk to that wedding planner. Mia is probably going out of her mind."

BRIGHT AND EARLY the next morning, Zane held open the door of Thayer's Jewelers, and ushered Storm inside. She stopped in the entryway and scanned the brightly lit store.

"Wow—it's got everything."

She was right. Mia Matheson and Rose Johnson had recently bought the place together. Now in addition to jewelry, Rose exhibited her artwork and Mia ran her wedding planning business here.

Mia came out of a small office to one side of the showroom. She was short, slim, with dark hair pulled back in a high ponytail. She stopped dead when she spotted them. "Zane Hall—am I finally meeting your bride?"

"You are."

Mia extended a hand. "I'm so happy to finally meet

you, Kenna. I'm Mia Matheson. I've been trying to reach your assistant for weeks. Isn't her phone working?"

Storm blushed and Zane bit back a curse. He should have seen that coming. "Actually," he said, "This is Kenna's assistant—Storm Willow. I'm marrying her instead."

"Oh…well…" Mia seemed nonplussed. "I… uh… okay. We'll have to redo a couple of things."

"I'm so sorry. I should have let you know. I meant to call you," Storm said.

"No problem. I'm sure things were… uh… chaotic." Mia blushed. "I mean… not to say that your decision to marry was chaotic…"

"It was," Zane said. "It still is. In fact, we might need to change the wedding date."

"You have got to be kidding," Mia blurted. She clapped a hand over her mouth. Struggled to compose herself. "I mean…"

Zane couldn't blame her for losing her temper. "Unfortunately not. It's a crazy story. I won't bore you with it."

"Please—bore us. We love crazy stories." Rose Johnson appeared from a back room, a petite pixie of a woman with dark hair curling around her face. As always, she exuded good cheer and Zane relaxed a bit. He liked Rose's friendly, matter-of-fact personality and felt like she was just the person to make this awkward experience easier for both him and Storm. Everyone said Rose was a whiz at helping people pick out the perfect engagement ring. In fact, he'd heard a rumor last time he came to visit that there was supposed to be something mystical about her. Zane cocked his head. She'd never looked mystical to him.

"Do you want to tell it or should I?" he asked Storm.

"You tell it. I'm going to look around."

"Great, abandon me at my time of need."

"You're a big, tough Marine. You'll get through it." She reached up to kiss him, then moved away to look at the art hanging on the wall.

"Go on," Rose said, leaning on a countertop. "We're all ears."

"Well, it started like this…"

"YOU'LL STILL NEED an engagement ring, even if you do have to delay the wedding," Rose said when Zane stopped talking. Storm, who was bent over a display case of engagement rings, shot her a conspiratorial smile.

Somewhere a baby began to cry. "I'm coming, Emily," Mia said. "Let me make the changes I need to make and I'll stop by the ranch to show you everything I've got planned," she said to Storm, heading into her office.

"I can't wait to see it all," she said.

Mia shut the door behind her, but they could hear her crooning nonsense words.

"Mia brings her baby to work," Rose explained. "Beats babysitters, at least for now; once Emily starts crawling we'll have to figure something else out." She moved behind the display case Storm was looking into. "Did you have something specific in mind?"

Zane touched Storm's back. "Something beautiful, just like my girl here."

Just like my girl.

Storm closed her eyes, basking under his attention. When she opened them again her gaze fell immediately on a delicate ring that reminded her of something a fairy would wear. It would look lovely on her slim fingers and she'd feel beautiful wearing it.

Before she could even point to it, Rose opened the back of the case and pulled it out. "Here you go."

Prickles danced down Storm's spine. How had Rose known which one she wanted?

"Try it on," Rose urged when Storm made no move to do so.

"Hold on." Zane took the ring. "She can't just put it on. We've got to do this right."

He got down on one knee and Storm's heartbeat quickened. She heard Rose gasp and saw Mia hurry out of the office and come to stand beside her friend, her baby in her arms.

"Storm." Zane took her left hand and held the ring to her finger. "I'm beginning to feel like Fate delivered you to me. Not in my wildest dreams could I have imagined the way my fiancée would come into my life. Now I can't imagine spending a day without you. All I do is for you. My land, my ranch, my work, my home, my heart—it's all for you. I want you to turn to me whenever you need for anything. I want you to know that I'll be there for you until my dying breath. I need you to know that if we have to start all over again, I'll gladly do it. It doesn't matter where we live. All that matters is that I get to wake up beside you each day for the rest of my life. I love you, Storm Willow. Please, would you be my wife?"

Tears pricked Storm's eyelids and for a moment she couldn't speak. She could only nod. "Yes," she finally gasped out. She was trembling as he slid the ring home.

When he stood up and pulled her into a soul-searing kiss, she felt as if the floor had fallen away beneath her. She clung to him as if to a lifeline, wondering how she had ever survived without him.

Maybe he was right; maybe Fate had delivered her to him. Maybe every moment in her life had led up to this one. She knew she was meant to be in Chance Creek. Meant to own a store. Meant to be with Zane.

Meant to wear this ring.

When they finally parted, Zane bent over her hand to get a better look. "Looks as if it was made for you."

"It does," Mia said, craning her neck to see.

"Yes, it does," Rose said with a secret smile.

"I love it." Storm turned to Zane. "I love you."

Zane smiled and her heart throbbed in response. He slapped the counter. "We'll take it."

"AREN'T WE GOING home?" Storm asked when he led her from the store, but didn't head toward his truck.

Zane shook his head. "Not yet. We've got one more stop." He took her arm and walked along the sidewalk, turning the corner when they reached it.

Storm glanced up at him. "Are we going to Mandy's?"

"You got it."

"Why?"

"Shh. You'll see."

When they reached the store, he waited for her to fish her key out of her bag and unlock the door before he hustled her inside and locked it again behind him.

"Hey, what are you doing?"

"I'm convincing my woman to have no-holds-barred, dirty, cheap, workplace sex."

She giggled. "Really? That's your plan?" She scanned the store. "This isn't exactly romantic."

"Let me put it this way. Neither one of us is ever going to work in an office, so boardroom sex is out. My workplace smells like manure. I'll happily take you on a hay bale someday, but I'm afraid you'll find that's pretty scratchy. Back home, your sisters are bound to knock on our door the minute we get going. So store sex it is."

"Where?"

He looked around, his gaze resting on the large front plate glass window. "Not in full view of the street, anyway."

"Back room?"

"Fitting room!"

She allowed him to take her hand and tug her toward the rear of the store. "This is weird."

"This is fun," he corrected. "Wait. You need something to try on. Get out there and find the trashiest dress you can."

"Trashy? Why?"

"So I can rip it off of you, what do you think?"

She did as she was told, refusing to show him what she'd found until she changed into it. "Go away," she said, pulling the door closed on one of the fitting room cubicles. They were old fashioned, with space below and above the walls, but she told Zane not to peek and he obeyed her. A few minutes later, she flung it open again to show off her new outfit.

"Wow." Zane was positive the item had to be from the eighties. It was a denim dress shaped to hug her curves, with a zipper in front from the neckline to the waist in addition to one in back that was actually useful to get the dress on and off.

"What do you think?" she said, striking a pose.

"It'll be like scoring with a star from a vintage music video." He hooked an arm around her waist and pulled her back into the cubicle with him. Shutting the door, he leaned her up against one of the partition walls and began to kiss her. At first he knew she was having a hard time taking any of this seriously, but when he tugged the front zipper down a few inches, parted the denim and began to sweep kisses along her neckline, Storm relaxed and began to kiss him back. She lifted her arms over her head to grip the top of the partition while he tugged the zipper down even further. Now he could slide a hand inside her dress and caress a breast.

"I don't suppose you can do that trick," he murmured, sliding his mouth along the edge of her bra cup.

"This trick?" She let go of the partition, wriggled around inside her dress for a moment or two and handed him her bra. "I'm not sure I ever got that last one back."

"What are you saying?" he growled into her ear, then ducked down to take one pert nipple into his mouth.

"I'm saying... oh..." Storm leaned back and allowed him full access to her breasts, clearly enjoying what he was doing. He lifted her arms so she gripped the top of the partition wall behind her again, loving how that lifted her breasts, too.

She was magnificent.

When he skimmed his hands down her hips and under the hem of her dress, she sighed with pleasure and he found she wasn't wearing panties. He pushed her dress up over her hips and lifted her up, wrapping her legs around his waist. The pressure of her hot, damp core against the front of his jeans was too enticing. He kicked off his boots, reached down between them, unbuckled his belt and pushed down his pants and boxers, groaning when his hardness slipped free and came in contact with Storm's slick body. Stepping out of his pants, he settled her legs more firmly around his waist, entranced with how good she felt. Supporting her back, he bent down to lave her breasts, giving them the attention they deserved.

"I want you inside me," Storm moaned.

"Be patient," he said, bending back to his task.

"I don't want to be patient." Using her arms to lift herself up, Storm positioned herself so his hardness pressed against her core. Zane chuckled and gave in, allowing her to slide back down, pushing him inside of her. He moaned and moved with her, pressing all the way in, using his hands to guide her hips.

"Hang on," he said and began to move. Soon both of them were panting, and Zane's thrusts were bouncing Storm against the wall with a rhythmic slap. She arched back as he increased his pace, her dress parting to reveal her breasts, and as he pistoned in and out of her, she cried out, her release overtaking her. Zane bucked against her, gripping her hips and thrusting until he was spent. He caught Storm in his arms and held her tight. "Hell, woman. You are the sexiest thing."

She peppered kisses over his neck and collarbone. "I hope you don't think you're done, cowboy."

He laughed out loud. "Really? Not even a minute to rest?"

"Not even a minute. Let me down." She steadied herself as he pulled out of her and helped her regain her feet, peeped up at him from under her lashes, made sure her front zipper was undone all the way, then turned around and lifted her skirt up to her waist again. "How about this?" she said, bracing her forearms against the wall.

"Are you trying to kill me?"

"I'm trying to get you to make me scream. Are you man enough for the job or do you need to send for reinforcements?"

"Reinforcements, huh?" Just looking at her had made him hard again. "How about this? Does that feel like I need reinforcements?" he asked her, nudging against her from behind.

"That feels perfect."

This time Zane moved more slowly, giving them both lots of time to warm up again. Twining his arms around her waist, he took advantage of her unzipped dress to reach inside and lift her heavy breasts. He didn't know what it was about the weight of them that turned him on so much, but between that and the sweet curve of her bottom on display he was soon too caught up in their lovemaking to analyze it. He couldn't imagine a better feeling than pushing inside her, unless it was pulling out and doing it all over again.

This time as he increased his pace he got to feel the sway of her breasts in his hands. He enjoyed the push of her soft skin, then slid one hand down between her legs and swirled his fingers, rewarded with her soft cries. Thrusting hard and deep, he kindled the flame within him again into a hot fire.

Storm. His Storm. He wanted to hear her cry out again—wanted to know how good he could make her feel. He held her in place, thrust in and out and waited for that moment—

When she cried out, he came with her, overcome with sensation, love and need until he bucked into her again, grunting with each movement. When it was over, he could barely stand. He reached for the top of the cubicle and steadied himself, easing out of her slowly.

Storm turned in his arms and tucked herself against him. Zane reached down to kiss her, sliding one hand under her hair to cup the nape of her neck.

"I love you. I will always love you," he whispered.

"I will always love fitting room sex," she whispered back.

"Any time, honey. Any time."

CHAPTER TWENTY

A WEEK OF cold, wet weather kept everyone inside and suddenly the Hall, which had seemed so cheerful and bustling with life, now felt cramped and dark. They all did what they could. Regan and Ella bustled around keeping a fire roaring in the living room fireplace and cups of coffee and hot chocolate flowing in the kitchen. The men spent as much time in the barns on their chores as possible, Cheyenne enrolled the girls in the local school, and in the afternoons she and Storm took the girls with them to the store to help prepare for the grand opening. Still, everywhere he went, Zane found himself bumping into someone else. He knew it was only a matter of time before tempers flared, so when the sun came out and burned the worst of the wetness away one afternoon, he gathered all the kids and Storm and brought them out to the obstacle course.

"Are you sure?" Storm asked, looking uncertainly at the large log structures. "I don't think the girls can do this. It doesn't look safe."

"Sure they can. We'll help them all the way. You

and I will spot them."

He sighed with relief when Storm acquiesced. He knew a good workout would do them all a world of good—even Storm, who sometimes battled with morning sickness but generally felt good in the afternoon.

At first the girls just played on a few of the easier obstacles while Richard, who had come for the afternoon, raced ahead, doing the whole course. Storm hovered near her sisters, watching for any slip that might bring trouble, but after a while she began to relax and when Zoe challenged her to try the first obstacle—a set of wooden monkey bars—Storm accepted.

She climbed up the two rungs on the vertical supports to get in reach of the horizontal bars, took hold of the first one, swung out and grabbed the next and was over it in no time.

"Race you," Zoe said, and climbed onto the other set.

"Come on, Storm! You can beat her," Violet cried.

"Come on, Zoe!" Daisy cheered.

Laughing, Storm took a starting position and Zane counted down to a start. "Three, two, one—go!"

They were off in a flash, both going hand-over-hand as fast as they could. For a moment it looked like Zoe had the lead, but Storm put on a burst of speed and outpaced her.

"Storm won!" Violet danced around. For a moment, Zane was afraid Zoe might cry, but as the girl regained her breath, she elbowed Storm.

"I thought you were supposed to let your kids win."

"You aren't my kid. You're my sister. You're supposed to torment your sisters," Storm countered. She grabbed Zoe and began to tickle her. Zoe shrieked happily and tickled her back. In a few moments they were both in a heap on the ground, laughing.

"Sometimes I forget you're my sister," Zoe said when she caught her breath again. "You used to be just like Mom."

Storm's expression faltered. "Yeah, I know." She stood up and brushed herself off.

"You're different now, though," Zoe said.

"Oh yeah? How so?"

"You're more… yourself."

"Is that a good thing?" Storm ruffled her sister's hair. Zoe made a face and smoothed it down again.

"Yes."

Her phone shrilled in her pocket, interrupting the moment, and Storm jumped. She hadn't heard that ring-tone in weeks. It was—

Kenna.

She grabbed the phone from her pocket, accepted the call and quickly lifted it to her ear. Her heart pounded. This was her chance to convince Kenna—

"Hello? Storm? Are you there?"

"Kenna?"

"Finally! You can't believe what it took to get this call through."

"Kenna, where are—"

"Here's the thing. You'll have to take my place."

Storm held the phone out and looked at it in shock. Kenna had said that once before, back when Storm had first arrived in Chance Creek. She returned it to her ear.

"Your place? Where?"

"In the wedding! What do you think?"

Storm had the strangest sensation of déjà vu. She'd already had this conversation, weeks ago. "But—"

"I'll pay you double. Just tell Zane everything and marry him under your own name. I'll pay you sixty grand the minute I get my inheritance."

"But... why?" Storm thought she must be losing her mind. Or maybe Kenna was. She couldn't be sure.

The silence on the other end of the line lasted so long Storm thought she'd lost Kenna again, but before she could speak, her boss came back. "Okay, I guess this is a surprise. You'll never believe this. I fell in love. I'm getting married for real."

Storm had never heard Kenna sound so happy—or so human. She clutched the phone more tightly to her ear. "Are you serious?"

"Yes. I know, it's crazy—"

"Actually, I think it's wonderful. Congratulations!"

"But Zane... that cowboy..."

Storm groaned as she realized the extent of the damage she'd done by her early marriage to Zane. Kenna was going to be furious.

"Storm?"

She steeled herself. "There's a bit of a problem with that. I married him already. In your name."

Kenna sputtered. "How... when?"

"When I first got here. Look, it's not that bad—"

"Not that bad?" Kenna raged. "I'm marrying in three weeks. Sam's whole family will be there!"

"Calm down. We've already looked into getting it annulled, but the sooner you get here the better."

"If you ruin my wedding, you can forget the money!"

Storm grit her teeth. "You know what, Kenna? Keep your money. I don't need it anymore."

Kenna went quiet again. "You're not... quitting, are you? Because this isn't a good time. I need you. There's the wedding, and I have to shift my trip to the Andes, and there's another grant application—"

"I'm sorry," Storm said gently. "I'm staying in Montana. I'm marrying Zane and I'm about to open a women's clothing store."

For the first time since she'd known Kenna, Storm heard uncertainty in her boss's voice. "But you'll be my Maid of Honor, won't you? I don't have anyone else to ask."

Storm hadn't ever imagined she could feel sorry for Kenna, but she did now. "Of course I'll be your Maid of Honor."

Storm hung up several minutes later and faced Zane, who'd been watching her intently.

"Well?"

"She'll be here in a couple of days to do whatever it takes to annul the wedding. We'll be free and clear to marry."

Zane let out a whoop, picked Storm up, whirled her around and kissed her. "See? I told you everything would be all right."

"You were right. You're always right." She kissed him back.

ZANE WAS RELIEVED that in the end it didn't take much to dissolve a marriage that had never been consummated. With both parties swearing to that, it was only a matter of processing the paper work. He was assured it would be done in time for his wedding to proceed, and once Kenna was gone, he and Storm immersed themselves in wedding preparations.

Several weeks later, Storm's family flew back to California briefly, Storm to be Kenna's Maid of Honor, and all of them to pack their things to be shipped to Chance Creek. Zane knew taking leave of their house was hard on all of them, but he hoped knowing their new friends and family were waiting for them had made it easier to return home to the ranch without heavy hearts.

The weather grew colder as October slipped into November and a wild wind whipped up one night. The following day there was a real chill in the air.

Cheyenne shivered dramatically as Zane walked with the women and girls to the truck to drive them into town. They'd drop the girls off at school, and then he would help Storm and Cheyenne hang mirrors and fix a few last things at the store. The grand opening was approaching fast.

"I never thought I'd live in snow," Cheyenne said. "We'll have to do a little shopping, girls. Snow pants, hats, winter coats."

"Better do it fast," Zane said. "I have a feeling we're going to see snow soon."

Later in the morning, Belinda sought him out when the others weren't nearby.

"Zane? Do you have a moment?"

Zane straightened the last of the mirrors he'd hung up and turned to find her watching him. Storm had told him that when it was only women in the store, Belinda was just as raucous as the rest of them, but the minute he arrived he sensed she clammed up and kept out of his way.

"Sure, what's up?"

"It's Darren. He…" She hesitated, then seemed to gather up her courage. "He doesn't know I work here."

"Still?" How on earth could he not know? News about everything traveled this town at the speed of light.

"I've been keeping it a secret."

Something clicked into place in his mind. Whenever someone outside their family walked into the store she found a reason to slip into the back room, or at the very least kept her back turned while she worked on hanging things on the racks. She hadn't worked the tag sale, something he hadn't really thought about at the time. He'd always thought she was a little shy, but now realized she was actually hiding.

"What are you going to do when the store opens

tomorrow?"

"I don't know."

"Belinda, you have to tell him. He'll be furious when he hears it from someone else."

"He's going to be furious no matter what." She stared up at him helplessly. "I have to quit, and I don't know how to tell Storm. She's been so nice."

"You can't quit." Zane ran a hand over his jaw, taking a good look at her. He remembered how washed out she'd appeared the first time he saw her in the store. Since then she'd gotten her hair done in an attractive style and she never let her roots show anymore. Her clothes were clean and pressed and she was always working hard, even if she wasn't speaking to him. That she'd pulled herself together during her time working with Storm was no coincidence. He could tell Belinda looked up to her. He wasn't worried about Storm or the opening; she had plenty of help to make things run smoothly. He was worried about the woman standing before him. Her demeanor told him how things were for Belinda. He didn't know how to ask his question delicately. "Does he hit you?"

Her eyes widened. "Darren? No." She shook her head. "No, nothing like that."

"Then why are you so afraid of him?"

She sighed. He noticed she was twisting her fingers together, but when she saw the direction of his gaze she stopped. "He makes life... unpleasant."

"You mean he yells."

Her lips pressed together. "Yells. Slams doors.

Breaks things, sometimes."

"Which is all a pretty good substitute for hitting you, because it makes you feel like that's just around the corner."

Her eyes filled with tears. "He's not a bad man."

Zane controlled his tongue, barely. "You know he won't change unless you do."

"What do you mean?"

"I mean, if you quit today and go back home, then nothing is going to change. But if you keep this job and don't let him change your mind, then he'll huff and puff and make life unpleasant, but he'll have to change at some point. Because you'll have changed. You'll have your own income, for one thing."

She nodded vigorously. "It's really helped so far, having my own money. I can pay our bills on time. I won't have to keep asking him for the cash."

"And it means you'll have choices, too."

They stared at each other.

"Are you going to quit?" Zane asked.

"No." She stepped forward and touched his hand. "Thank you."

"All of us are here for you. Whenever you need us, okay?"

"Okay."

When she went back out into the main room, Zane stayed behind to think, afraid that trouble would come of this. He'd fill his brothers in on the situation, but apart from that he didn't know what he could do to head it off.

"OPENING DAY. I'M so proud of you, honey," Cheyenne said, giving Storm's shoulders a little squeeze as they stood outside and looked at the new sign that graced the store. After a lotof thought, Storm had decided to rechristen the establishment Heloise's in honor of the cantankerous old woman who'd brought her and Zane together. "The store looks beautiful. Women are going to be lining up to get their clothes here."

"I sure hope so," Storm said. She was proud of what she'd accomplished. She'd decided to start by focusing on clothing that the women around town could wear every day, with options for dressing up their outfits for going out on the town at night. The clothes were practical, yet she strove to ensure that every one of her outfits would be flattering, as well. She had decided not to partition larger sizes off to one area, either. Instead she stocked most items from petite through women's sizes.

Interspersed among the clothing she'd stocked decorative household items she found charming and exotic. Some were one of a kind. Others were manufactured, but all of them had flair.

Belinda had taken charge of the jewelry section and Storm loved the displays she'd set up around the checkout counter. Her mother had gravitated toward the boots and handbags. Together, Storm felt they made a terrific team.

Her one worry was Darren. Zane had told her about the conversation he'd had with Belinda on the topic and she knew it was only a matter of time before the man had it out with his wife. She hoped when he did, Belinda wouldn't back down.

"It's time," Belinda called. "Should I open the doors?"

"You bet," Storm said.

A moment later the first customers walked in and she didn't have time to worry anymore.

FOUR HOURS LATER, Storm was exhausted but pleased with the way her first day was unfolding. The women of Chance Creek certainly liked a novelty. The stream of customers had been almost constant since they'd opened. She knew that would subside in time and she'd have to be careful if she wanted to turn a profit, but with the rate women were purchasing her clothes, she felt that she had a hit on her hands.

She was handing a large shopping bag to a customer when Darren walked in.

"Uh-oh," she said.

Cheyenne looked up. "What's wrong? Are you out of change?"

"No, that's Belinda's husband."

"Uh-oh," Cheyenne echoed her. "I'll head her off."

It was too late. Belinda came out of the back room leading a customer who'd just tried on a stack of skirts and sweaters.

"I'm sure you'll be happy with the ones you picked out," she was saying when she spotted her husband.

"Grab the customer," Storm hissed at Cheyenne.

"I'll help Belinda."

As Darren and his wife faced off, Storm rounded the counter and came up beside her.

"Darren, don't make trouble," Belinda said.

"No need for trouble, as long as you're out that door in three seconds."

Storm didn't think he'd been drinking, for which she was very grateful. Alcohol could turn this confrontation into something serious in a matter of moments.

It looked like it was going to get serious anyway, though. She wished Zane was here. She wondered if she should call the police, but before she could move Darren grabbed Belinda's wrist. "I said go. Get in the truck."

"No. This is my job. I'm not leaving."

"Why would you work for the people who stole our home from us?"

All around the store, customers stopped browsing and turned to watch the argument.

"They didn't steal our home. Your father piddled it away." Belinda matched his volume and his tone. "He's the one to blame, Darren. He's the one that couldn't even bother to change his will and leave it to you. Why was that?"

"Because he was a bastard."

"That's what you always say. What if it was something else? What if he knew you hated ranching? What if he didn't want to saddle you with a property that would be a mill-stone around your neck?"

He looked confused. "I don't hate ranching."

"Are you serious? I've known you all my life, Darren Hall. I listened to you bitch about every last detail of working with cattle from the time we were in junior high. I cheered you on when you left the ranch, or have you forgotten that? We went out to the Dancing Boot and toasted your freedom!"

"Didn't work out too well, did it?" he said belligerently. "Construction doesn't pay enough."

"Which is why I'm working—to help out," Belinda pointed out.

"A man should be able to support—"

"How many men are supporting their families single-handed these days?" Belinda raked her gaze around the store and called out, "Raise your hands. How many of you are getting by on one income?"

One woman raised her hand timidly. "I'm a single mom," she said, then ducked behind a rack of clothing.

"See? It isn't the Hall boys, or your daddy that's the problem. It's your pride."

"Pride's all I got!"

"You know what? Zane's proud. Austin's proud. So's Mason. But you know what else they got? Family! Each other. Friends, too. That's what I want. I want to stop sitting alone in my house night after night because where we live or what we cook or how we dress isn't good enough for you. No one cares if we're tight on money. We have five children. We live in the modern world. Life is hard, Darren, but you're making it harder."

"You can't blame a man for wanting to hold his

head up. I want to feel like I've done something at the end of the day." His face was twisted with a pain Storm recognized all too well.

"You've done plenty." A woman Storm didn't know stepped toward Darren. "You came and fixed my fence for me last year when the neighbors' dog kept getting in and digging up my garden. I know that's not a big job for you, but it was a big deal for me. I freeze and can what I grow. We eat that food all winter long. You barely charged me for the work, either. I appreciated that more than I could say."

"You helped my parents last year, too," another woman said. "Pat and Sarah Fullman on the east side of town. You fixed their roof in the middle of that awful week of rain we got last October. Got it patched up before the damage spread too far. They're on a fixed income. They might have had to sell their home if it weren't for you."

"Remember when my Cynthia moved home with her two kids four years back?" a third woman stepped forward. "We didn't know where we were going to put them. We'd already downsized. You built that basement suite for them for half of what the other contractor quoted us. Two bedrooms and a bath. Cynthia still talks about that, even though she's married again and moved back out. Now we have a place to put guests when they come to stay."

Darren stepped back as the compliments kept coming, as if he was spooked by the positive attention. Belinda took his hand, basking in the other women's approval. When the stories began to die down, she said, "See? I wouldn't marry a man who wasn't wonderful."

"I—well, I…" Darren scanned the room. Caught sight of the door. "I'll be back at closing time." He hurried away and disappeared outside. Belinda faced the customers.

"Thank you. All of you. That meant a lot to me."

With murmured assurances that what they'd said was true, the women began to return to their browsing. Belinda fluttered around the room to help. Cheyenne returned to Storm's side.

"That went better than I'd expected."

"I wouldn't have believed it if I hadn't seen it."

"You know, I'm beginning to really like this town," Cheyenne said.

WHEN ZANE CAME to pick the women up at the end of the day, they were celebrating with mock champagne, and to his surprise Darren was holding his plastic glass up for a toast along with the rest of them.

"To your first day," he was saying to Storm as Zane walked in.

"Hear, hear," Cheyenne said and drunk hers down.

Darren lowered his glass as Zane approached. "Hey there, Zane."

"Darren."

Zane looked around at the women's happy faces, and noticed that Darren had Belinda's arm tucked through his. He didn't know what kind of magic Storm had wrought, but he decided he wouldn't be the one to undo it, as much as he still wanted to know if Darren was behind the cut in the pasture fence or Mason's flat tire. He could see that Belinda and Storm were thrilled that Darren was behaving himself. It would be churlish of him to rock the boat.

"What do you think of the store?" he asked his cousin.

"I think it's great. Belinda did the jewelry displays." He lifted his chin as if daring Zane to put his wife's efforts down.

"I didn't know that. They look great, Belinda. And you…" He dropped a kiss on Storm's nose. "Look fantastic for a hard-working entrepreneur. Ready for some dinner?"

"Should we all head to DelMonaco's?" Belinda asked.

"That sounds like a good idea," Storm said. "Is that okay, honey?" She linked her arm with Zane's.

"That's just fine."

On the way out to their vehicles Zane managed to get Darren to the side. It was one thing to share a toast, but it was another to share an entire dinner with a man who might have been making mischief on his property. "We've had a few problems around the ranch lately."

"Oh yeah? What kind of problems?"

"Mason's tire was punctured."

Darren grimaced. "Some damn kids slashed one of my tires, too, last month. Someone ought to give them a whupping."

Zane frowned. "One of our pasture fences was cut,

too."

Darren swore. "That's going too far. You don't mess with a man's livelihood. Need help repairing it?"

Zane was too shocked to answer. Darren wanted to help?

A look of understanding came into Darren's eyes. "Oh, I get it. You think I'm behind your problems."

"Looks like I was wrong," Zane said. "I'm glad to know it."

Darren ducked his head. "You weren't wrong about all of it. I did get Steel to hit on Storm at the Dancing Boot. That was just for a laugh, though. I didn't mean for it to turn into a fight."

"Yeah, well, Steel's in charge of himself, I reckon."

"Hope he didn't scare Storm."

Zane shook his head. "No, it all turned out okay." He had to suppress a grin when he remembered how that night had ended. In his own messed up way, Darren had helped him and Storm become a real couple.

"See you at the restaurant," Darren said and walked off.

"See you there."

Hours later, when they were finally alone together in their room, Zane took his time undressing Storm. "How on earth did you persuade Darren not to be mad at Belinda?" He eased off her shirt and kissed her shoulder.

"I didn't do a thing. Belinda surprised the heck out of me. He came in like thunder, demanding that she leave and she put him right in his place."

"And he wasn't furious?" He trailed kisses across her back to the other shoulder. Storm unstrapped her bra and let it drop. He slid his hands around her to cup her breasts.

"He didn't have time to be. She was too busy telling him what a wonderful husband he was."

Zane snorted.

"No, really, and what's crazy is all these women in the store came forward to tell stories about what he'd done in the past that had helped them. Turns out he's done a lot."

"Huh." He thought about that. "Good for him."

"Belinda pointed out that he didn't like ranching but that he was good at his job, and that if they were both working they'd be okay."

"She's a smart woman." He resumed kissing her, this time pressing his lips to her neck.

"She is." Storm turned in his arms. "Enough about Darren and Belinda."

"More than enough," Zane said. Lifting her up, he deposited her on the bed and soon followed, stripping his clothes off as he went.

"I don't suppose this will be half as exciting as fitting room sex," she said, pulling him close.

"Oh, yeah? We'll see about that." He wrapped his arms around her and rolled over, ending with her straddled across his lap. "Exciting enough for you?"

"Heading in the right direction," she said.

"Hmm. I think you're heading in the wrong direction, actually." He guided her to turn around so she was sitting facing away from him. "That's better." When she took him in her hands, sliding them up and down his hardness, he let his head fall back and groaned.

"You like that."

He made an indeterminate noise and she chuckled. "I'll take that as a yes."

Zane scooted back to prop himself against the headboard, then skimmed his hands up over her waist and down over her hips. When she lifted herself and settled down again, taking him inside slowly, he let out the breath he was holding, gratified as always by how good she felt. As she rose and fell on her knees, the view of her body was enough to make it sweet torture. With the delicious sensation of her slick folds sliding over him, it was enough to make it hard not to lose control.

He guided her up and down with his hands, then slid them upward to cup her breasts. Sliding his thumbs over her nipples, pinching and caressing them, he could tell Storm was turned on by the way she moved. He skimmed his hands down again, captured her wrists and held them behind her while she rose and fell on top of him, encouraging her by the tilt of his hips.

Storm moved faster, each movement exposing her body to his view. He kept his grip on her wrists, imagining the jut of her breasts as her back arched and her breathing quickened.

"Zane." Her tone told him all he needed to know

and he moved faster as she slid up and down. When she cried out he was close behind her, the sound of his name on her lips all he needed to crash over the edge and come with a violence that had his head spinning.

Storm kept moving until both of them were spent. When he released her wrists, he sat up to take her into his arms.

"I will never get tired of making love to you."

"I will never get tired of you inside of me," she said, looking over her shoulder.

"Come here."

Storm eased off of him and burrowed down beside him under the covers. He traced a finger down her arm and up again. "Did I ever tell you how glad I am you're not a mountain climber?"

"No." She chuckled. "Why don't you want me to climb mountains?"

"Because I don't want to lose you."

"You won't. You're stuck with me." She rolled on top of him again.

"You have no idea how happy I am to hear that."

CHAPTER TWENTY-ONE

"**I** STILL CAN'T believe you asked me to be one of your bridesmaids," Belinda said as she came out of the changing room in the back of Ellie's Bridals in her sky-blue gown. Ella and Regan lined up next to her and together they struck a pose. "I love it that you're including your sisters, too. They look so cute in their junior bridesmaid dresses."

Storm had always known she'd have her sisters in her wedding when she married, but they were still so young she'd decided she needed a grownup set of bridesmaids, too. Austin and Mason would stand up with Zane, with Richard as a young counterpart to the three girls.

Ellie, the owner of the store, bustled into the fitting room area and clapped. "Those dresses are so elegant."

"And they're not pretending to be anything other than bridesmaid's gowns," Regan said. "I hate it when people try to make them usable again for other occasions. It never works!"

"I'm not pretending this occasion is anything other than it is—a big, ol' awesome western wedding," Storm said. "I'm a modern woman in every way, but I always wanted an old-fashioned wedding. Big white dress, big white cake, dancing…"

"Don't forget cowboy boots." Ella tugged up the hem of the beautiful gown that Storm had tried on to show her boots underneath.

"Well, that goes without saying," Belinda said. "What kind of bride doesn't wear boots?" She kept her face straight until the other women exchanged a look, then laughed at them. "I'm just kidding. Although I did wear boots to my wedding. I'm a country girl through and through."

"I think I'll wear them too," Storm said. "As a sign to Zane that I mean to stay here. That I love it here."

"That you love him," Regan added.

"That I love him," Storm agreed.

"So that's three of you," Belinda said. "Who will Colt bring home, I wonder?"

"I hope he doesn't bring anyone," Storm said. "I hope he falls back in love with Heather."

"Everything is so good right now on the ranch I don't want anything to change." Ella posed in front of the mirror. "What if Colt brings someone new home that we all hate?"

"Don't even say that." Regan joined her. "Anyway, why borrow trouble? Come here, Belinda." She held out a hand and pulled Belinda into place beside them. Storm joined them, standing in the middle. "Look at us. Aren't we a picture?"

Ellie pulled a cell phone out of her pocket and

snapped a photo. "Yes, you are."

"THREE WEDDINGS IN one year," Zane's mother said when she arrived at the Hall. Zane helped carry her bag indoors and up the stairs to the third-floor room she'd use for the duration of her stay. He'd put her next to Cheyenne, hoping they'd get along and knowing his mother would enjoy the company of the girls down the hallway.

"I can't wait for you to meet Storm."

"She seems like a darling girl."

"We've got some news, too."

"Tell me." She sat down on her bed and looked around the small room. "How strange it is to be up here where I used to put guests."

He was instantly beside her. "Do you want us to move you downstairs? We can shuffle people around. I just thought—"

"Shh, it's perfect. I simply miss it here."

"As soon as Heloise gives us that deed, we'll come to Florida to collect you," he assured her.

"I can't wait. But I can't live with you in the Hall. And Austin's taken the bunkhouse."

"We'll figure it out," Zane assured her. "You belong here as much as we do. We'll find a way that suits everyone."

"What's your news?"

"Be prepared to welcome another Hall baby in May or so. Storm's pregnant."

"You boys. Can't even wait to get properly married,

can you?" But she was beaming with happiness. "Grandchildren. I'm going to have oodles of grand-children." She looked at him archly. "Mason said you had a little trouble along the way to getting Storm to be your wife, but you got her in the end, didn't you."

"What Gunnery Sergeant Zane Hall wants, Gun-nery Sergeant Zane Hall gets," he said with satisfaction.

"What on earth are you talking about?"

"Nothing, Mom." He dropped a kiss on her head. "Glad you're here."

A DUSTING OF snow covered the ground on Thanks-giving and Storm was glad the Hall was so cozy. Her wedding would consist of an afternoon ceremony at the Chance Creek Reformed Church, and a catered dinner to follow at the Hall. The furniture had been removed from the large living room and replaced by small clusters of chairs and tables around an empty space reserved for dancing. Austin had put together a song list with Regan and Ella's help and they'd wired the living room for sound, as well.

Mia Matheson helped in a million ways and Storm was glad to have her nearby as she primped for a final time in a small room at the church while all her new friends and family took their seats.

"You're as pretty as a picture," Mia said, fluffing out her veil. "It's fun to watch the Hall boys bring home their brides. It's fun to see you all working together the way we do at the Double-Bar-K, too."

"This is a pretty special place." Storm met her gaze

in the mirror.

"That it is. Come on. I think they're nearly ready for you."

As she moved to leave her room, her mother met her in the doorway. "Mia, could you give us a minute?"

"Of course."

As soon as they were alone, Cheyenne pressed an envelope into Storm's hand.

"What's this?"

"Open it." Cheyenne smiled.

Storm tore open the envelope and pulled out a check. A shock ran through her at the amount it was made out for. "Mom—you didn't need to do this."

"I don't need to buy you a ranch, so I'm giving you this instead. A nest egg."

"It's too much."

"No, it isn't," Cheyenne said firmly. "Eight years of work, that's what this signifies. Eight years of putting off your dreams to allow me the time to mourn my husband. What mother ever had a better daughter? I wish I could give you that time back, honey, but I can't. This is all I can do."

"I'll start a college fund for the baby. And order in the best stock for my store anyone could imagine. People will be coming from California to shop there."

"I bet they will. I'm so proud of you."

Tears pricked Storm's eyes. "What about you? Are you happy?"

"Happier than I've been in a long, long time."

As the first chords of the wedding processional

rang out in the church, Mia returned and beckoned Storm to take her place beside Hank, who had volunteered to walk her down the aisle. She took hold of his arm, trembling with emotion at what Cheyenne had done, but it was the cowboy at the end of the aisle who held her attention now. Zane stood strong and proud beside his brothers and Richard, waiting for her. Love and happiness swelled in her chest as she stepped toward him, and she couldn't think of anywhere she'd rather be than in this country church, with this community she'd grown to love so much.

Near the altar, Zane watched her approach, beaming at her with pride and happiness until she fell in love with him all over again. As she joined him in front of the minister, Hank put her hand into Zane's.

Zane squeezed it, his eyes telling her how much he loved her. She hoped he could read the depth of her love in hers.

"Dearly Beloved," the minister began, and Storm's heart filled to bursting.

She was right where she belonged.

CHAPTER TWENTY-TWO

"HERE'S TO COLT," Mason said, lifting a glass of champagne many hours later. Most of the guests had gone home after a wonderful meal of traditional Thanksgiving fare and vegetarian alternatives, followed up by dancing. Zane was happier than he could say with Storm pressed close to him, knowing as he did he'd have a full week alone with her.

"To Colt," the others answered, clinking their glasses together. Storm's was filled with a non-alcoholic champagne substitute, but she was as flushed and happy as everyone else.

"I hope he gets in touch soon," Regan said. "I can't get used to this lack of communication."

"Just part of the job," Austin said. "Wish he was here, though."

"Me, too."

"Here's to Heloise for bringing all of us together," Ella said suddenly. "That woman is a pain in the ass, but she's done a good thing here."

"I'll toast to that," Zane said. He checked his watch. "And it's time for us to go, Mrs. Hall."

"I'll get my things," Regan said with a saucy grin.

"I'll get my things, too," Ella said. "A week in New Orleans sounds like just the ticket."

"Sorry, ladies. I'm only taking Mrs. *Zane* Hall on this particular honeymoon."

"And since this is the only honeymoon *Mr.* Zane Hall is ever taking, you're out of luck," Storm added pertly. She stood up and held out a hand to her husband. "Besides, I don't think we'll be very good company."

"Nope."

But as they drove off in the limousine hired to take them to the airport, Storm looked over her shoulder out the back window at Crescent Hall blazing with light, and found herself already anticipating their return in a few days' time.

The ranch had become her home.

THE END

The Heroes of Chance Creek series continues with The Airman's E-Mail Order Bride.

Read on for an excerpt of Volume 1 of **The Cowboys of Chance Creek** series – *The Cowboy's E-Mail Order Bride*. Please note that this novel is not part of the Heroes of Chance Creek series; it is the first in the earlier series, The Cowboys of Chance Creek.

Visit Cora Seton's website and sign up for her Newsletter here. Find her on Facebook at facebook.com/CoraSeton.

OTHER TITLES BY CORA SETON:

THE HEROES OF CHANCE CREEK:

The Navy SEAL's E-Mail Order Bride (Volume 1)
The Soldier's E-Mail Order Bride (Volume 2)
The Navy SEAL's Christmas Bride (Volume 4)
The Airman's E-Mail Order Bride (Volume 5)

THE COWBOYS OF CHANCE CREEK:

The Cowboy's E-mail Order Bride (Volume 1)
The Cowboy Wins a Bride (Volume 2)
The Cowboy Imports a Bride (Volume 3)
The Cowgirl Ropes a Billionaire (Volume 4)
The Sheriff Catches a Bride (Volume 5)
The Cowboy Lassos a Bride (Volume 6)
The Cowboy Rescues a Bride (Volume 7)
The Cowboy Earns a Bride (Volume 8)
The Cowboy Inherits a Bride (Volume 9)

The Cowboy's E-Mail

Order Bride

BY CORA SETON

Chapter One

"**Y**OU DID WHAT?" Ethan Cruz turned his back on the slate and glass entrance to Chance Creek, Montana's Regional Airport, and jiggled the door handle of Rob Matheson's battered red Chevy truck. Locked. It figured—Rob had to know he'd want to turn tail and head back to town the minute he found out what his friends had done. "Open the damned door, Rob."

"Not a chance. You've got to come in—we're picking up your bride."

"I don't have a bride and no one getting off that plane concerns me. You've had your fun, now open up the door or I'm grabbing a taxi." He faced his friends. Rob, who'd lived on the ranch next door to his their entire lives. Cab Johnson, county sheriff, who was far too level-headed to be part of this mess. And Jamie Lassiter, the best horse trainer west of the Mississippi as long as you could pry him away from the ladies. The four of them had gone to school together, played football together, and spent more Saturday nights at the bar than he could count. How many times had he gotten them out of trouble, drove them home when they'd had one beer to many, listened to them bellyache about their girlfriends or lack thereof when all he really wanted to do was knock back a cold one and play a game of pool? What the hell had he ever done to deserve this?

Unfortunately, he knew exactly what he'd done. He'd played a spectacularly brilliant prank a month or so ago on Rob—a prank that still had the town buzzing—and Rob concocted this nightmare as payback. Rob got him drunk one night and egged him on about his ex-fiancee until he spilled his guts about how much it still bothered him that Lacey Taylor had given him the boot in favor of that rich sonofabitch Carl Whitfield. The name made him want to spit. Dressed like a cowboy when everyone knew he couldn't ride to save his life.

Lacey bailed on him just as life had delivered a walloping one-two punch. First his parents died in a car accident. Then he discovered the ranch was mortgaged to the hilt. As soon as Lacey learned there would be some hard times ahead, she took off like a runaway horse. Didn't even have the decency to break up with him face to face. Before he knew it Carl was flying Lacey all over creation in his private plane. Las Vegas. San Francisco. Houston. He never had a chance to get her back.

He should have kept his thoughts bottled up where they belonged—would have kept them bottled up if

Rob hadn't kept putting those shots into his hand—but no, after he got done swearing and railing at Lacey's bad taste in men, he apparently decided to lecture his friends on the merits of a real woman. The kind of woman a cowboy should marry.

And Rob—good ol' Rob—captured the whole thing with his cell phone.

When he showed it to him the following day, Ethan made short work of the asinine gadget, but it was too late. Rob had already emailed the video to Cab and Jamie, and the three of them spent the next several days making his life damn miserable over it.

If only they'd left it there.

The other two would have, but Rob was still sore about that old practical joke, so he took things even further. He decided there must be a woman out there somewhere who met all of the requirements Ethan expounded on during his drunken rant. To find her, he did what any rational man would do. He edited Ethan's rant into a video advertisement for a damned mail order bride.

And posted it on YouTube.

Rob showed him the video on the ride over to the airport. There he was for all the world to see, sounding like a jack-ass—hell, looking like one, too. Rob's fancy editing made his rant sound like a proposition. "What I want," he heard himself say, "is a traditional bride. A bride for a cowboy. 18—25 years old, willing to work hard, beautiful, quiet, sweet, good cook, ready for children. I'm willing to give her a trial. One month'll tell me all I need to know." Then the image cut out to a screen full of text, telling women how to submit their video applications.

Unbelievable. This was low—real low—even for Rob.

Ready for children?

"You all are cracked in the head. I'm not going in there."

"Come on, Ethan," Cab said. The big man stood with his legs spread, his arms folded over his barrel chest, ready to stop him if he tried to run. "The girl's come all the way from New York. You're not even going to say hello? What kind of a fiance are you?"

He clenched his fists. "No kind at all. And there isn't any girl in there. You know it. I know it. So stop wasting my time. There isn't any girl dumb enough to answer something like that!"

The other men exchanged a look.

"Actually," Jamie said, leaning against the Chevy and rubbing the stubble on his chin with the back of his hand. "We got nearly 200 answers to that video. Took us hours to get through them all." He grinned. "Who can resist a cowboy, right?"

As far as Ethan was concerned, plenty of women could. Lacey certainly had resisted him. Hence his bachelor status. "So you picked the ugliest, dumbest girl and tricked her into buying a plane ticket. Terrific."

Rob looked pained. "No, we found one that's both hot and smart. And we chipped in and bought the ticket—round trip, because we figured you wouldn't know a good thing when it kicked you in the butt, so we'd have to send her back. Have a little faith in your friends. You think we'd steer you wrong?"

Hell, yes. Ethan took a deep breath and squared his shoulders. The guys wouldn't admit they were joking until he'd gone into the airport and hung around the gate looking foolish for a suitable amount of time. And if they were stupid enough to actually fly a girl out here, he couldn't trust them to put her back on a plane home. So now instead of finishing his chores before supper, he'd lose the rest of the afternoon sorting out this mess.

"Fine. Let's get this over with," he said, striding toward the front door. Inside, he didn't bother to look at the television screen which showed incoming and outgoing flights. Chance Creek Regional had all of four gates. He'd just follow the hall as far as homeland security allowed him and wait until some lost soul deplaned.

"Look—it's on time." Rob grabbed his arm and tried to hurry him along. Ethan dug in the heels of his well worn boots and proceeded at his own pace.

Jamie pulled a cardboard sign out from under his jacket and flashed it at Ethan before holding it up above his head. It read, Autumn Leeds. Jamie shrugged at Ethan's expression. "I know—the name's brutal."

"Want to see her?" Cab pulled out a gadget and handed it over. Ethan held it gingerly. The laptop he bought on the advice of his accountant still sat untouched in his tiny office back at the ranch. He hated these miniature things that ran on swoops and swipes and taps on buttons that weren't really there. Cab reached over and pressed something and it came to life, showing a pretty young woman in a cotton dress in a kitchen preparing what appeared to be a pot roast.

"Hi, I'm Autumn," she said, looking straight at him. "Autumn Leeds. As you can see, I love cooking…"

Rob whooped and pointed. "Look—there she is! I told you she'd come!"

Ethan raised his gaze from the gadget to see the woman herself walking toward them down the carpeted hall. Long black hair, startling blue eyes, porcelain-white skin, she was thin and haunted and luminous all at the same time. She, too, held a cell phone and seemed to be consulting it, her gaze glancing down then sweeping the crowd. As their eyes met, hers widened with recognition. He groaned inwardly when he realized this pretty woman had probably watched Rob's stupid video multiple times. She might be looking at his picture now.

As the crowd of passengers and relatives split around their party, she walked straight up to them and held out her hand. "Ethan Cruz?" Her voice was low and husky, her fingers cool and her handshake firm. He found himself wanting to linger over it. Instead he nodded. "I'm Autumn Leeds. Your bride."

AUTUMN HAD NEVER BEEN more terrified in her life. In her short career as a columnist for CityPretty Magazine, she'd interviewed models, society women, CEO's and politicians, but all of them were urbanites, and she'd never had to leave New York to get the job done. As soon as her plane departed LaGuardia she knew she'd made a mistake. As the city skyline fell away and the countryside below her emptied into farmland, she clutched the arms of her seat as if she was heading for the moon rather than Montana. Now, hours later, she felt off-kilter and fuzzy, and the four men before her looked like extras in a Western flick. Large, muscled, rough men who all exuded a distinct odor of sweat she realized probably came from an honest afternoon's work. Entirely out of her comfort zone, she wondered for the millionth time if she'd done the right thing. It's the only way to get my contract renewed, she reminded herself. She had to write a story different from all the other articles in CityPretty. In these tough economic times, the magazine was downsizing—again. If she didn't want to find herself out on the street, she had to produce—fast.

And what better story to write than the tale of a Montana cowboy using YouTube to search for an email-order bride?

Ethan Cruz looked back at her, seemingly at a loss for words. Well, that was to be expected with a cowboy, right? The ones in movies said about one word every ten minutes or so. That's why his video said she needed to be quiet. Well, she could be quiet. She didn't trust herself to speak, anyway.

She'd never been so near a cowboy before. Her

best friend, Becka, helped shoot her video response, and they'd spent a hilarious day creating a pseudo-Autumn guaranteed to warm the cockles of a cowboy's heart. Together, they'd decided to pitch her as desperate to escape the dirty city and unleash her inner farm wife on Ethan's Montana ranch. They hinted she loved gardening, canning, and all the domestic arts. They played up both her toughness (she played first base in high school baseball) and her femininity (she loved quilting—*what an outright lie*). She had six costume changes in the three minute video.

Over her vehement protests, Becka forced her to end the video with a close-up of her face while she uttered the words, "I often fall asleep imagining the family I'll someday have." Autumn's cheeks warmed as she recalled the depth of the deception. She wasn't a country girl pining to be a wife; she was a career girl who didn't intend to have kids for at least another decade. Right?

Of course.

Except somehow, when she watched the final video, the life the false Autumn said she wanted sounded far more compelling than the life the real Autumn lived. Especially the part about wanting a family.

It wasn't that she didn't want a career. She just wanted a different one—a different life. She hated how hectic and shallow everything seemed now. She remembered her childhood, back when she had two parents—a successful investment banker father and a stay-at-home mother who made the best cookies in

New York City. Back then, her mom, Teresa, loved to take Autumn and her sister, Lily, to visit museums, see movies and plays, walk in Central Park and shop in the ethnic groceries that surrounded their home. On Sundays, they cooked fabulous feasts together and her mother's laugh rang out loud and often. Friends and relatives stopped by to eat and talk, and Autumn played with the other children while the grownups clustered around the kitchen table. All that changed when she turned nine and her father left them for a travel agent. Her parents' divorce was horrible. The fight wasn't over custody; her father was all too eager to leave child-rearing to her mother while he toured Brazil with his new wife. The fight was over money—over the bulk of the savings her father had transferred to offshore accounts in the weeks before the breakup, and refused to return.

Broke, single and humiliated, her mother took up the threads of the life she'd put aside to marry and raise a family. A graduate of an elite liberal arts college, with several years of medical school already under her belt, she moved them into a tiny apartment on the edge of a barely-decent neighborhood and returned to her studies. Those were lean, lonely years when everyone had to pitch in. Autumn's older sister watched over her after school, and Teresa expected them to take on any and all chores they could possibly handle. As Autumn grew, she took over the cooking and shopping and finally the family's accounts. Teresa had no time for cultural excursions, let alone entertaining friends, but by the time Autumn was ready to go to college herself, she ran a successful OB-GYN practice that catered to wealthy women who'd left childbearing until the last possible moment, and she didn't even have to take out a loan to fund her education.

Determined her daughters would never face the same challenges she had, Teresa raised them with three guiding precepts:

Every woman must be self-supporting.

Marriage is a trap set by men for women.

Parenthood must be postponed until one reaches the pinnacle of her career.

Autumn's sister, Lily, was a shining example of this guide to life. She was single, ran her own physical therapy clinic, and didn't plan to marry or have children any time soon. Next to her, Autumn felt like a black sheep. She couldn't seem to accept work was all there was to life. Couldn't forget the joy of laying a table for a host of guests. She still missed those happy, crowded Sunday afternoons so much it hurt her to think about them.

She forced her thoughts back to the present. The man before her was ten times more handsome than he was in his video, and that was saying a lot. Dark hair, blue eyes, a chiseled jaw with just a trace of manly stubble. His shoulders were broad and his stance radiated a determination she found more than compelling. This was a man you could lean on, a man who could take care of the bad guys, wrangle the cattle, and still sweep you off your feet.

"Ethan, aren't you going to say hello to your fiancee?" One of the other men stuck out his hand. "I'm Rob Matheson. This is Cab Johnson and Jamie Lassiter. Ethan here needed some backup."

Rob was blonde, about Ethan's size, but not nearly so serious. In fact, she bet he was a real cut-up. That shit-eating grin probably never left his face. Cab was larger than the others—six foot four maybe, powerfully built. He wore a sheriff's uniform. Jamie was lean but muscular, with dark brown hair that fell into his eyes. They had the easy camaraderie that spoke of a long acquaintance. They probably knew each other as kids, and would take turns being best man at each other's weddings.

Her wedding.

No—she'd be long gone before the month was up. She had three weeks to turn in the story; maybe four, if it was really juicy. She'd pitched it to the editor of CityPretty as soon as the idea occurred to her. Margaret's uncertain approval told her she was probably allowing her one last hurrah before CityPretty let her go.

Still, just for one moment she imagined herself standing side by side Ethan at the altar of some country church, pledging her love to him. What would it be like to marry a near stranger and try to forge a life with him?

Insane, that's what.

So why did the idea send tendrils of warmth into all the right places?

She glanced up at Ethan to find him glancing down, and the warm feeling curved around her insides again. Surely New York men couldn't be shorter than this crew, or any less manly, but she couldn't remember the last time she'd been around so much blatant testosterone. She must be ovulating. Why else would she react like this to a perfect stranger?

Ethan touched her arm. "This way." She followed him down the hall, the others falling into place behind them like a cowboy entourage. She stifled a sudden laugh at the absurdity of it all, slipped her hand into her purse and grabbed her digital camera, capturing the scene with a few clicks. Had this man—this...*cowboy*— sat down and planned out the video he'd made? She tried to picture Ethan bending over a desk and carefully writing out "Sweet. Good cook. Ready for children."

She blew out a breath and wondered if she was the only one stifling in this sudden heat. Ready for children? Hardly. Still...if she was going to make babies with anyone...

Shaking her head to dispel that dangerous image, she found herself at the airport's single baggage carousel. It was just shuddering to life and within moments she pointed out first one, then another sleek, black suitcase. Ethan took them both, began to move toward the door and then faltered to a stop. He avoided her gaze, focusing on something far beyond her shoulder. "It's just...I wasn't...."

Oh God, Autumn thought, a sudden chill racing down her spine. Her stomach lurched and she raised a hand as if to ward off his words. She hadn't even considered this.

He'd taken one look and decided to send her back.

ETHAN STARED INTO THE STRICKEN EYES of the most beautiful woman he'd ever met. He had to confess to her right now the extent of the joke she'd been led into thinking was real. It'd been bad enough when he thought Rob and the rest of them had simply hauled him to the airport for a chance to laugh their asses off at him, but now there was a woman involved, a real, beautiful, fragile woman. He had to stop this before it went any further.

When she raised her clear blue gaze to his, he saw panic, horror, and an awful recognition he instantly realized meant she thought she'd been judged and found wanting. He knew he'd do anything to make that look go away. Judged wanting. As if. The girl was as beautiful as a harvest moon shining on frost-flecked fields in late November. He itched to touch her, take her hand, pull her hard against him and...

Whoa—that thought couldn't go any farther.

He swallowed hard and tried again. "I...it's just my place...something came up and I didn't get a chance to fix it like I meant to." She relaxed a fraction and he rushed on. "It's a good house—built by my great granddaddy in 1889 for the hired help. Solid. Just needs a little attention."

"A woman's touch," Rob threw in.

Ethan restrained himself, barely. He'd get back at

all of his friends soon enough. "I just hope you'll be comfortable."

A snigger behind him made him clench his fists.

"I don't mind if it's rough," Autumn said, eliciting a bark of laughter from the peanut gallery. She blushed and Ethan couldn't take his eyes off her face, although he wished she hadn't caught the joke. She'd look like that in bed, after…

Enough.

"Give me the keys," he said to Rob. When his friend hesitated, he held out a hand. "Now."

Rob handed them over with a raised eyebrow, but Ethan just led the way outside and threw Autumn's suitcases in the bed of the truck. He opened the passenger side door.

"Thank you," she said, putting first one foot, then the other on the running board and scrambling somewhat ungracefully into the seat. City girl. At least her hesitation gave him a long moment to enjoy the view.

Rob made as if to open the door to the back bench seat, but Ethan shoved him aside, pressed down the lock and closed the passenger door. He was halfway around the truck before Rob could react.

"Hey, what are you doing?"

"Taking a ride with my fiancee. You all find your own way home." He was in the driver's side with the ignition turning over before any of them moved a muscle. Stupid fools. They'd made their beds and they could sleep in them.

He glanced at the ethereal princess sitting less than two feet away. Meanwhile, he'd sleep in his own comfortable bed tonight. Maybe with a little company for once.

ABOUT THE AUTHOR

Cora Seton loves cowboys, country life, gardening, bike-riding, and lazing around with a good book. Mother of four, wife to a computer programmer/eco-farmer, she ditched her California lifestyle nine years ago and moved to a remote logging town in northwestern British Columbia.

Like the characters in her novels, Cora enjoys old-fashioned pursuits and modern technology, spending mornings transforming an ordinary one-acre lot into a paradise of orchards, berry bushes and market gardens, and afternoons writing the latest Chance Creek romance novel on her iPad mini.

Visit www.coraseton.com to read about new releases, locate your favorite characters on the Chance Creek map, and learn about contests and other cool events!